DEAR MR. CAPOTE

ALSO BY GORDON LISH

What I Know So Far
Peru
Mourner at the Door
Extravaganza
My Romance
Zimzum
Selected Stories
Epigraph

DEAR MR. CAPOTE

Gordon Lish

A NOVEL

FOUR WALLS EIGHT WINDOWS
NEW YORK / LONDON

© 1983, 1996 BY GORDON LISH

PUBLISHED IN THE UNITED STATES BY
FOUR WALLS EIGHT WINDOWS
39 WEST 14TH STREET
NEW YORK, N.Y. 10011

U.K. OFFICES:
FOUR WALLS EIGHT WINDOWS/TURNAROUND
27 HORSELL ROAD
LONDON N51 XL

FIRST CLOTH EDITION PUBLISHED BY HOLT, RINEHART AND WINSTON
IN 1983. FIRST PAPER EDITION PUBLISHED BY SCRIBNER SIGNATURE
EDITIONS IN 1986. FIRST FOUR WALLS EIGHT WINDOWS PAPER
EDITION PUBLISHED IN 1996.

ALL RIGHTS RESERVED.
NO PART OF THIS BOOK MAY BE REPRODUCED, STORED IN A DATABASE
OR OTHER RETRIEVAL SYSTEM, OR TRANSMITTED
IN ANY FORM, BY ANY MEANS, INCLUDING MECHANICAL, ELECTRONIC,
PHOTOCOPYING, RECORDING, OR OTHERWISE, WITHOUT THE PRIOR
WRITTEN PERMISSION OF THE PUBLISHER.

LIBRARY OF CONGRESS CATALOGUING-IN-PUBLICATION DATA:
LISH, GORDON.
DEAR MR. CAPOTE: A NOVEL/GORDON LISH.
P. CM.
ISBN 1-56858-079-7 (PBK)
I. TITLE
PS3562.174D4   1996
813'.54—DC20   96-25820
CIP

PRINTED IN THE UNITED STATES
TEXT DESIGN BY INK, INC.
10 9 8 7 6 5 4 3 2 1

CHICAGO PUBLIC LIBRARY
LITERATURE AND LANG... ...VISION
LITERATURE INF... ...CENTER
400 S... STATE STREET
...ICAGO, ILLINOIS 60605

FOR HELEN DEUTSCH
AND OUR ADELE
AND TO KATHRYN BELDEN

DEAR MR. CAPOTE

THIS IS THE TWELFTH START of the letter I am sending. Here is the reason it's the twelfth start. The reason is to try out voices! I want the right one. Granted, they sound like the right one for a while. But is a while long enough? It is like years ago when I did a voice for fifteen minutes, time out for commercial announcements. I am making reference to my former profession on the radio, a quarter hour for each voice.

Sometimes two in less than that.

Nothing's changed. I know how long a minute is.

Here are some of the starts I tried.

Dear Mr. Capote, Effectuate a good grip on your socks! Get ready to shake, rattle, and roll! Is this your lucky day or is this your lucky day?

Dear Mr. Capote, Please listen. All I am doing is begging for you to listen. Listen, *effectuate* is one of the words so far.

Dear Mr. C., You know who this is? Answer: This is the person who can make a certain writer millions if a certain writer plays his cards right, which I do not have to tell you is not what a certain Mr. Norman Mailer did!

Dear Mr. Capote, With your permission, I will go ahead and introduce myself. Hint: I am the one who is killing the people. Correction: Just the ones which when Nature calls sit down to you-know-what.

Dear Mr. Capote, Credit where credit is due. I do not have to suck up to someone in your circle. I myself am in the papers and also on all of the channels. I am a household word. I am the party which Gotham looks for, except name me the Gothamite who is (joke) using both eyes for them to do it, ha ha. All right, I ask you—who has Gotham scared shitless, Norman, me, or you?

Dear Mr. Capote, Call Random House! Tell them to clear the deck, stop the presses, whip out their checkbook and start practicing zeros!

Dear Mr. Capote, In all humility, I am already more famous than you are even if in the public nobody knows my name by heart. But I say do not try skipping to the sign-off to find it yet. Reason: It is not there yet (joke) because I'm not, ha ha.

Dear Truman, Norman had the ball, I handed him the ball, and he muffed. But do I have to tell you why? Okay, too many children! Believe me, I am familiar with the situation. It is the one a man with children gets in. So this in a nutshell is my personal analysis, take it or leave it. Whereas present company is clean as a whistle in the department I just made mention of. Granted, this is why I should be horsewhipped for picking Mr. M. in the first place.

Dear Mr. Capote, It is my pleasure to inform you respective to the fact that this letter is germane to the legalized disposition of the media rights pursuant to my story, it being lawfully agreed I shall deem it correct and acceptable to authorize you to deliver aforesaid story to the public in accordance with the terms set forth herein.

Dear Mr. Capote, It's all right, admit it. Hint: You knew you were next in line. So where else could yours truly go, considering? There is Norman Mailer, you bet, but is this individual still a legitimate factor? Let's face it, the nervy s.o.b. played himself right out of the picture!

THAT WAS TEN OF THE STARTS. The other one I tore up. Correction: Eleven, not counting the one I am doing now, which is No. 12.

Listen, do me a favor and don't ask me what the missing start was. Between you, me, and the lamppost, it is not overly important. The major thing is proof. Here it is. What I say I am is one hundred percent the facts. This is a person which is reliable talking.

The other thing of it is, forget it, all the business about the different voices. Meaning, I have to talk the way I talk. But the thing is, I don't overdo it. Let's face it, everything is a question of the right word in the right place so long as the right one (joke) starts out being the wrong one, ha ha.

Capstone, for example, that's another one of the words. But which one is it?

I go between five-nine and five-eleven. God is my judge, you can depend on it. Granted, right-handed is also the situation as far as which handed.

You know as well as I do this is what the media is

guessing. Or let's say the authorities the media is quoting. But these are the only two guesses which come anywhere close. Okay, the police figure five-six to five-seven on account of "angle of entry." Whereas the right-handed part comes from the fact of which eye the knife gets in. I know I don't have to tell you, it's the left one!

But forget it. Because the rest of the guesses they are guessing they are way off base about.

Hey, take my word for it! (Ha ha.)

So all in good time, okay? Meaning, when it comes to what's what, you will be the first to know. For example, going back to radio, check it out—Ann Shepherd's real name was Scheindel Kalish.

Here is another one. Ann Shepherd (S.K.) was also Hope Evans on *Big Sister.*

Look it up if you don't believe me. Go ahead and look it up all you want. You think if yours truly says it, it does not check out from top to bottom?

Okay, the media is saying I am crazy and dangerous. But these are the two biggest things they are wrong about. I do not have to tell you they are all wet from the word go. So what if I was put away once? This was when? We are talking about the age of sixteen! Forget it. You know how old I am right this minute? Forty-seven! I said forty-seven. So how's that, forty-seven and no further episode has befallen me since the one I just made mention of!

I know what you are thinking. You are thinking he is

already all balled up. This is because I said you were going to be the first to know but meanwhile said I already told Norman. So which means any way you slice it, present company is second! Is this what you are thinking, or is this what you are thinking?

Well, I did. But let's face it, sometimes an individual has to wait his turn, even a famous celebrity. So who is the one which really regrets it? Listen, do not make me laugh. You know as well as I do, Norman had his chance. But what he did is took me for a fool. Which is what I was when it was him I wrote to instead of to you. So let's say I was jumpy and not thinking things through. Meanwhile, the dumbest part is how I go for a family man. Whereas let's say I wasn't thinking things through by my Number One rule. If I was, would I touch a family man with a ten-foot pole?

This is my first major rule—think a thing all of the way through. Because I say you have not thought it through enough when you come out on the same side you started on. Okay, this is something else I'm going to get to. Sit tight. I am going to get to everything.

Listen to this. If you live long enough, there is nothing you are not going to.

Here is a fact. I am a thorough type of individual. One thing I do not do is leave a thing out. So okay, I left out a thing here and a thing there when I wrote to you-know-who. But just between you, me, and the lamppost, it is not true it was because I forgot. In other words, I had to.

Here is something else. I go slow. It is the lesson I learned going all of the way back to Janet R.'s bathroom. Go fast and get balled up. Go slow and stay one hundred percent. So this is the second major rule.

Not that I do not know what it is for the people who have to listen. I know how they don't want to and how they can't wait for me to speed it up. But this is the voice I have and, I'm sorry, I have to go slow with it. Hey, look at what happened to Bobby R.? Meaning, Mr. C., feel free if you have to skip. Okay, I give you permission to take a peek at the sign-off—except, ha ha, if you really did it, it wouldn't be there yet if you did!

ALL RIGHT, YOU CAN TELL what I am doing—you can see that I am stalling. It is because I am jumpy and can't catch my breath yet. This is the start I cannot take a chance to make a mess of. I do not have to remind you what number start this is. Not that I believe in superstitiousness. It is just that there is no reason for you to risk what you don't have to.

You are saying he is crazy because he is killing so many people. Whereas I say you are saying this because you have not thought it through yet. But even if I was, we could still do business. Being crazy is no impediment to doing business.

Impediment. That was another one of the words I used so far, *effectuate* and *impediment* and *capstone.* Like this: "Impediment."

You'll see.

Here is another one. Ann Shepherd was also Pearl Taggart on *Our Gal Sunday*. In other words, Scheindel Kalish was!

Okay, I am catching my breath. My thoughts are getting collected. But before I get down to cases, I have to straighten out some things so far.

Number One) If I sometimes don't follow my rule and always don't go slow enough, it is because of Norman and of what he is doing right this minute. I know how long a minute is!

Number Two) I said all the channels, but not on 13 here in Gotham—"The Big Apple" being an expression I have nothing but disdain for. *Disdain,* by the way—this is another one of the words from the word-calendar which I bought for the boy a birthday ago.

Number Three) I have nothing but disdain for all of the other channels. This is not due to my years on the radio and what the television did to me. This is because Channel 13 is the serious channel!

Number Four) I say years even though I know as well as the next one months is all it was. Years is, so to speak, a manner of speaking.

Number Five) There are twenty-three so far. So if yours truly is forty-seven, you can guess how many I have to go before I am all finished. Meaning, I am writing to you at the stage of me not being over halfway there yet.

Norman I wrote to when I was up to twelve. This was because I did not want to get in touch with him until he could see I am a serious person. But by now there is no question if I am, okay?

Number Six) The wife watches 2, 4, and 7, whereas the boy and me stick to Channel 13. I don't have to tell you I do not let him watch the others because what are the others but blood and guts? Do the others ever teach you anything? I am very picky about this. I do not want the boy not to know the things I didn't and vice versa. T.C.'s the wife, and she says I am too conscientious, whereas I say a person can't be. This is why the boy has the calendar and also the walkie-talkie. You understand what I mean, the Word-a-Day calendar? The words come from there, whereas where yours truly comes from is from the seven-watter.

Number Seven) They are just beginning to make mention of me on 13 now that I am up to so many individuals. Hint: One more than Berkowitz! It is on *Newsline*, Catherine Campion reporting. She is pretty. In my personal opinion, Catherine Campion looks like Janet R., especially if you look at the hair. But T.C. says watch 2 and see Sue Cott. She says Cott leaves the other one in the dust.

Number Eight) T.C. stands for Tamara Chris, the ball and chain for the last ten big ones—also for seven more of "keeping house" before we tied the knot. Not that I wouldn't leave T.C. in two seconds flat if Janet R. showed up. I would take the boy and go.

Number Nine) You are probably wondering why I am only doing it to women. Stop wondering. Here is the answer. Better targets. Bigger eyes. Correction: I don't need both of them.

But I am being ridick to say a thing like this, Number Eight above. I cannot take the boy and go. This is because of the whole point of the thing, which is get to forty-seven and then get caught. On the other hand, no one is going to catch anyone until yours truly comes to terms with a certain famous author.

Three guesses who this person is!

Hint: He is not Mr. Norman Mailer!

I know I do not have to tell you I would be honored and thrilled if you took over. But I also do not have to tell you I negotiate on behalf of the boy, and when I do anything on behalf of the boy, it is a big mistake for somebody to get cute with me. Which I do not have to tell you is what a certain Mr. You-Know-Who did. I promise you, he is the one who is crazy if he thinks I got an idea like this just to get it all balled up at the last minute. "Last minute" is a manner of speaking.

All right, I am not in the business. Granted, I am just a beginner when it comes to making things happen in the media. But I am the father of the boy, and the father of the boy is no pushover!

No offense intended. Believe me, I don't like to shout. But I guarantee you, the boy is the one subject yours truly gets touchy on. This particular subject aside, no individual is a milder individual. Name anybody, and I will meet this party halfway, Mr. Mailer included. Listen, I may be killing lots of people, but not for some mean or ridick reason.

I will tell you how to think about me.

Think about me as being an inventor who is selling his invention. Don't think about me as a Bundy or a Berkowitz. I am nine million miles from individuals of that type. I am a fellow who knows what he has to work with and is working with it. In this day and age, you tell me where the choice is.

In other words, this is for the boy! This is for the big bucks! This is the boy's dad talking, who is your solid American citizen from soup to nuts!

Okay, here are the facts.

I am dependable. I work in a top-ten bank. Seventeen years I have been in the same position. Seventeen! Ask anyone. You can check it out with my immediate supervisor. My immediate supervisor will give you every assurance everything I tell you is one hundred percent. I am aboveboard as the day is long.

Here is an example.

Peartree's.

Gives you a scare, doesn't it?—Peartree's.

All right, so I know about you and Peartree's, corner of First and Forty-ninth.

You'll see. I know a lot.

I even know the bartender's name, which is Gary. I don't drink, but I know the name. I always order soda. Can you beat it? Liquor salesman's son, but does he ever touch a drop?

I never eat there, either. I guess I do not have to tell you what the reason is. No offense. You can afford it. I say more power to you because you can. On the other hand, you are keeping an eye on your waistline. I know. I watch. I say an individual has a right to do this. I mean, to keep his tummy flat. This is one of the things about T.C. Hers is not the way it was when we started out. Hint: It used to be like Janet R.'s, only now it's not!

I guess this makes you sweat, me knowing things about you and where you go and so on.

I know it does.

Believe me, I am a sensitive person to what another person feels. I know what it is like to be a famous celebrity and have other people know things. Let's face it, aren't I a famous celebrity now myself?

I mentioned Peartree's to make a point. I could walk over and show you what I use. But I respect your privacy. Anyway, I could. I could let you see Paki for yourself. I could put my hand down on the bar and lift it up and let you look. You would see the knife. Personally, I do not think you would try to brush me off. I make a good impression. I used to be an actor. Granted, it was on the radio and nobody saw me. But my appearance is okay. I am neatly dressed. I know how to behave with famous celebrities. I also have a way with words. My manners are without impediment. I know how to say something. I mean a word that makes you stop and stare. *Impediment,* for instance. And what about *capstone?*

In other words, I think you would have given me my due. Given my due, I could have told you the plan right then and there. We could have worked the deal face-to-face. You would have seen what I use when I do it. You could have seen Paki with your own (joke) two eyes, ha ha. Sure, I can give you the mental picture, but the mental picture is just a picture!

So why didn't I do it at Peartree's?

Here is the answer.

It's a mystery to me too.

I AM GOING TO START with how I got Paki.

I found it. I never would have had the nerve to buy one. Does this seem outlandish to you, considering? But it is one hundred percent, I swear. Knives make me afraid. It could be because of when I was little and went into Simon's or it could be because of something else. I don't know. Maybe buying knives just scares people. Maybe buying knives does this, whereas who can say why?

Not that knives scared her. She could be in a place with knives. She could say, "I'll only be a minute," and be in a place hours and hours with knives. Or I could be on the television and have enough money instead.

Just think. Suppose I did not have to negotiate. Suppose the boy was taken care of. Suppose the future was all set. I could be like every other fellow who walks into Peartree's and sees the famous celebrity. I could say, "Have a drink on me." We would be two famous celebrities shooting the breeze. I could show you Janet Rose's snapshot and you could show me one of yours. We could talk about me and you being on the television.

But I never even got back on the radio after I was you-know-where. So where is the money going to come from?

Meanwhile look at what is happening to the future. Do I have to tell you what they are saying? The facts are the facts! Meaning, the future which is coming up is going to be the worst future we ever had. And I don't have to tell you that's the one the boy is going to be in!

It is enough to make you sick, everybody in the whole future worse off than the one we're having right now.

Let's face it, this was the United States Government talking—they said it, they said it!—and for your information, a certain person was listening with both ears.

So now you have the reason.

Here it is again.

The boy does not have a chance!

It is like his three-speed against a tenner no matter how hard he pedals. It is like what is the good of the Word-a-Day calendar and his learning all of the words. Or me making the rule against him watching the wrong channels.

You see why I am using the knife?

The type is the folding type. Here is the mental picture. When the blade is back in the handle, Paki comes to four and three-quarter inches, which means almost double when the blade is out.

This is when you see PAKISTAN stamped where the steel or the metal of it is.

It got me wondering when I saw it. You just never stop to think if they make hard things in a place like that, like Pakistan and so forth and so on. I thought it was only baskets they made and other soft things, period.

The other thing is, turn the blade over. That's when you see this.

13030.

Here is the truth. I don't like looking at this number. It makes me get a little sweaty.

WHEN I WAS LITTLE, everything made me a little sweaty. But this is just the word I use. Meaning, as a person, my skin is on the dry side.

It didn't happen until Buddy Brown.

Getting sweaty, I mean.

I don't know. I can't explain it.

Up until we moved, I was the happiest boy there was. She was always saying I was out of this world. This is how happy I made myself—and made everybody else because I was. Just looking at me made the people feel good.

Tell the truth. Weren't you a boy like that?

She said I was a picture-book boy. But what did she say after she saw Buddy Brown move in next door? Did she say picture-book boy anymore?

I thought everything loved me. I thought the sky and trees and clouds loved me. I thought the sky wanted to reach down its arms down and hug me. I thought everything wanted to grab me and squeeze.

Okay, I lied. Meaning, even before Buddy Brown, I sometimes got a little sweaty. Here's why—if things loved me so much, maybe they were going to get me and keep me!

This is the reason I did not go out unless she made me. It wasn't safe outdoors. Whereas inside, it was a little less jumpy and sweaty.

If it was raining and I had to play in the house, saved is how I felt. You know what I thought? I thought I was saved for one more day. I thought outside I'd get taken away. I thought the sky would come and get me.

So I tried to stay indoors. This is how I first made up the voices. In other words, I said I was sick. Then I got a voice to go with it, whichever sickness I said it was.

Strictly for the sake of argument, let's say it was sunny. This meant go out and play. But I said I hurt somewhere and I made up the voice to prove it. Also, here is the face if you are looking. But the thing of it is afterwards. Do you see what I am saying? I mean, the voice and face I just made up. I mean, even if nobody is listening or looking, the voice and face stay right where they are. Here's why. Because I am here where I am. Because I see, I hear.

Let's face it, where Mr. M. is concerned, you keep your mouth shut about things like this. Am I right or am I right? Because, come on, look at him.

So this is how sunny days I stayed inside. Which is also how I saw the dust. It was the dust between us. I mean, between her and me.

Here is the mental picture.

It was when she was sewing. Listen, I don't have to tell you this is what I loved.

We had venetian blinds. We had them in both houses, the first one and the second. She is sitting in the chair, whereas I am on the hassock. There is this window that is behind her, the slats fixed for just the exact angle. In other words, when you have a needle and thread, you need plenty of light to go with it.

Now here is the thing. The light lights up the air!

Maybe the light was different in that day and age. I mean, maybe the light was brighter or a different color. Because I ask you, have I seen the specks since?

I did not know they were dust, okay? No one ever told me they were dust, okay? This is something I had to find out. But did anyone tell me when I saw?

They glittered! They jumped! They switched direction like a wave!

You see what I mean about breathing? This is how thick it is when you breathe.

But here is the point. I thought they were little animal things. I thought they flew around in the air. I did not think you-know-who would laugh.

It was like when I used to listen to the motor. This is the motor when she is cleaning with the vacuum. Before she went to business, she was always sewing and cleaning with the vacuum. So here she comes cleaning with the vacuum, and I hear like voices in the noise. You know what they're doing? They are saying my brother's name!

It was just like with the specks I thought were animals. Meaning, I thought everybody heard them. So why make mention if she didn't? Granted, she laughed. But wasn't this because they switched direction?

You can see the child I was. But in my personal analysis, every child is.

Hey, so you tell me. Believe me, I'm listening with both ears. For me it was the specks and in the motor of it. So what was it for present company? I'll bet you thought of some things yourself. You just forget, that's all. Guess what. If I heard you mention your things, I would think, "Hey, wait a minute, what's that? That's ridick!"

This is just human nature. Am I right or am I right?

Actually, I know some of your things. Let's face it, you have made reference in your bestsellers. But did I laugh?

Meanwhile, now is the time for you to laugh if you have to. T.C. does. It's okay if you have to. But here it is.

I used to think there were little people in the radio. But I say so what? It was just my parents didn't tell me.

Here's a thought. Maybe they didn't know. But I say even if your parents know everything, there is going to be something nobody stops you from thinking. So big deal! Let us not kid ourselves, by the time you are of a certain age in years and so on, you are in the know.

The boy, for example. He knows how to work the walkie-talkie. "You copy, Red Dog? This is Blue Dog, over and out."

Guess who that was on the seven-watter.

You see? Face facts. The boy is only nine! But he is almost in it already. Meaning, in the know.

Hey, you can thank the Word-a-Day calendar for a lot of it. And let's not forget him watching the right channel!

TIME OUT. I JUST THOUGHT OF SOMETHING. It is another place where I was maybe less than one hundred percent in the first place. But I'll bet you would have caught me at it anyway without me even telling you.

It's this. I said why it is strictly women only. In other words, your range of females. I said it was the bigger eyes which is the reason. But let's not forget there are these other things, which is these things like this—mascara and eye shadow and eyeliner and eye pencil and sometimes your cream and your glitter.

Another thing is the extra lashes.

You see what I mean when I say target?

Here is something. It's easier to hit it with it. It's like the archery concession at Coney Island, rings and rings around the black spot in the center. The difference is, this is Paki, here comes Paki, get set for Paki, it's Paki!

But it's hard to hit it. Ask T.C.

Hint: She calls it a part of the Devil's body. But does the Devil really have one?

Anyway, it's the size of that, the Devil's heel, more or less.

Here is something else. Where your female is concerned, one eye is bigger than the other. In my personal experience, this is the case, whatever they tell you otherwise.

So go ahead. Guess which one it is. Except don't bother.

I mean, talk about your lucky breaks!

So what if I was born left-handed? Did you ever stop to think about this? Listen, I do all the time.

Here is one more thing so long as this is the subject which we are talking about. Okay, so far it is just a theory. But for what it's worth, this is my analysis.

With your woman, the brain is closer!

So what do you think? I mean, you think you can use it or not? Or is it crazy?

On the other hand, don't hold me to anything. I mean, when you do the book, take it easy. I say don't put it down until you check it out. Let's face it, with material like this, we're dopes if there is something we don't get one hundred percent! But just so you don't forget to check it out, make yourself a note. True or false: From the eye to the woman's brain the distance is shorter than the man's brain is.

Enough said?

Hold it. I just thought of one more thing. What about when they wear contacts? I didn't tell you about when they are wearing them, contacts. In other words, if they've got on glasses, forget it. But when it's not glasses but contacts, who knows?

You see what I am getting at?

With the pigeon-toed one which was the first one, was this the sound I thought I heard, true or false? I mean, the click. You know, Paki clicking on one of her you-know-whats when Paki clicked on it?

SO WHEN I WAS A LITTLE YOUNGER than the age the boy is now, I was always waiting for something to grab me. This is why I locked the car doors when you-know-who made me shop with her. I'm talking about back before she went to business. To make a long story short, she was always parking somewhere and also in a hurry. So she leaves me in the Plymouth because it's faster when I am. In other words, she says it's faster if she goes by herself.

She says, "I'll only be a minute."

But she never is. I don't think she ever was. It is more in the neighborhood of more than fifteen, to I would say, to thirty minutes. Whereas the time at Simon's, I don't know, maybe double or more than double this.

Granted, I know as well as the next one it is just a manner of speaking, "I'll only be a minute." But when it was happening, it was like the specks and like the radio. I mean, nobody told me what a minute is. You understand what I am saying? It's just dust and waves. But how do you know if they don't tell you?

I knew it wasn't long. This is how I figured I could wait it out. But then I couldn't. I would try and try, but then it got to be too much longer than I thought it was going to be, and who could hold it anymore? So then I would lock the doors and get on the floor.

Listen, I do not think I would hold it against him if the boy did that. Let's face it, we don't have a car. But I don't think I would. The thing is, I would be all for it if he did, seeing as how Safety First is one of my major rules.

The boy is nine. Yet I say you cannot be too careful.

As for yours truly, seven is the age I am talking about— and you can quote me on that.

Here is how I know.

Seven was the most important age in my life!

Seven was the year we moved.

Seven was when my dad went with the liquor company, so we had the Plymouth there at home, whereas him they gave a special vehicle to to drive around with and to sell the liquor from. This is one thing I can tell you. I was seven when we changed houses—and when we did it, everything else changed too.

Number one, we moved. Number two, guess who came to live next door.

SOMETHING HAPPENED BECAUSE of Buddy Brown. The same thing goes because of Simon's. I can't say what did. But it was something.

Simon's was the hardware. Here is as far as this.

One day she goes, "I'll only be a minute." It was a nice day. I think it was October after school. I don't have to tell you I felt good. This is the time of the year I do. Let's say it makes me think of Janet R. walking. But back when I was seven, I don't know. Maybe it was the leaves or the light or the colors or being seven.

I was sitting in the seat watching all of the people. That's a thing I really like. Meaning, seeing people through the glass. So as bad as it is to be in the Plymouth, it isn't so bad at the start. And then it comes to me how it's so amazing, my head. This is because I have stopped counting for what a minute is!

Okay, you are going to have to think back to when you were the age I was. Norman couldn't, but I know you could. So think back and you tell me, am I right or am I right? I mean, you do something you didn't think you could, okay? And then what? So you see what I mean?

It's like you get so proud you tremble!

Say you are a young individual and people are always telling you how you are going to outgrow this, that, or the other thing. But do you believe it for a minute? For example, he was always telling her how I will outgrow locking the doors. And then, bingo, you outgrow it! Because there

I am, and I know it has to be way more than a minute is. But did I lock the doors and get on the floor?

Hey, here's the truth—I was really trembling. It made me tremble the way I was just sitting there and still looking at all of the people. Even now, here in Gotham in this kitchen, you think I can't see the boy I was and how I was trembling in the Plymouth?

Listen, I was trembling. It was wonderful.

But then it's getting dark, and she's not back at all. So it keeps getting darker, and I can see how the people on the sidewalk are starting to look cold and going-home-looking. You see what I'm saying when I say they did? They are not shopping now. They are leaving places and getting going-home-looking and looking cold.

So I just had to do it. I tried hard not to. But it was no use. It was like having to go to the bathroom. It was like squeezing and squeezing to stop it. But then you can't. And you start knowing here it comes. So this is when I get the feeling I mean when I get sweaty.

But meanwhile I am looking all around. In other words, she must be coming and I want to see where she must be coming from. Granted, sometimes I was more or less in a position to make a guess. For example, she maybe says, "I'm just going into the market," or "I'm just going into the dimestore," or "I'm only going to pick up a few drug items for a minute, and I'll only be a minute."

But sometimes all she does is go, "I'll only be a minute."

So I get so sweaty, I can't remember what she said. Meaning, did she or didn't she give me a hint? This is when I get up on my knees and keep turning my head around to see. It is also when I think if I lock the doors and spot her coming, I can get them open again before she sees they aren't. In other words, who's to say I didn't outgrow it? Because didn't I really?

The next thing is, even looking around is no good. It's too dark. I can't see unless it's close. The only thing is the lights inside the stores and where there are the darknesses of the people in the ones which have some windows.

It was terrible. It was the sweatiest time I ever had up until the time of Buddy Brown.

I ask you, would an individual like a Norman Mailer see what I am saying? Would your Norman Mailer type of individual put it in when it came time to write the book? Now I see how it was just wasting my breath to give him the background material. You know what? I think it lowered me in his eyes. Whereas in yours it doesn't do that, true or false?

So now there is this second thing, which is this. I was afraid to lock the doors! I know it's crazy, but I am more sweaty about her catching me locking them than I am about me still waiting in the car. Here is when I have to squeeze the hardest, and then I let go and push the door.

I ran. Across the sidewalk and into the first store.

It was Simon's.

It was the hardware.

I was never in it before. I was never in any place anything like it before. Never anywhere had I ever smelled
anything like what it smelled like in Simon's before.

It had long aisles. Everything all over was all stacked up.
You couldn't see around them. You couldn't see anyone
anywhere anymore. You couldn't see her. All you can see
are the things and the things on the shelves.

I keep looking up for her.

Then I look down.

Then this is when I see it right in front of where I am.

It was a case. It was maybe the size of this table. What is
in it is under the glass.

I am talking about the knives!

But none of them was like this one. Paki is streamlined.
The handle is streamlined so you can hold it and it fits.

The thing of it is, I do not remember the next thing
after that. I can't tell you if she was there in Simon's or
how she got me home. I just remember looking at them
and how they looked under the glass.

Here's something.

Only over my dead body will the boy ever see a thing
like that!

BUT WHO KNOWS WHAT YOU are going to see? If you
live long enough, there is nothing you don't. For example,
what happened on Fourteenth.

Last year I was down there. It was just before Christmas.

Believe me, I know better. Fourteenth Street, nobody has to tell you what's doing in a neighborhood like this. But I was checking out a thing for the boy, which was a bicycle, to make a long story short. Let's just say I was shopping all over Gotham for the best buy for the money.

Okay, you are a person in your circle, so you don't know about buys to begin with. But take it from me, in this day and age it is a scandal what they get for something in this particular department. Especially with gears, if this is what the doctor ordered.

The boy wanted one with gears. The truth is, he did. Even if he said he didn't. I don't have to tell you he was just saying no because of the money. You see the point I am making? In my household, everybody knows money and safety are the two categories.

Let's face it, he's only in the fourth grade, but the boys in the classroom are getting bikes with gears galore. This will interest you. Make a special note. Much as you will not believe it, by the fourth grade even your coloreds are pedaling around on tenners! Even your colored girls are.

I don't have to tell you what a ten-speed goes for in the world of today. We are talking about an item that is in a whole different department than your item with not one gear to its name.

So T.C. decides we meet the boy halfway. Which is when I go out to see what we can do on a three-speed. It is a Saturday and I am all over Gotham checking. But who am I kidding? I mean, the one place to go is the place way over west on Fourteenth, which is nothing but bicycles wall-to-wall. You never saw anything like it! So I go over and I ascertain the prices. Okay, they are high. But let's not forget the advantage of service! Also, if something goes haywire, you can bring it back and get satisfaction. In other words, you have your year's guarantee—in writing—which I make mention of because of how come present company got to be a famous celebrity, right? So I am making up my mind in the right direction when it comes to me in a flash. May's! Meaning, you've got to be crazy to sign on the dotted line without first checking out the situation at May's.

You would not know because of your circle. But I am here to tell you, May's is a store at Broadway and Fourteenth. Face facts, this places it right in the vicinity! So you get the picture. I got to walk how many blocks to save a dollar? Believe me, you could double it and yours truly is not complaining!

Granted, May's is not in the business of catering to a person of your level. But I say whoever you are, it makes sense to save a dollar! Besides, it's ridick to be in the vicinity and not see if at May's I can't do better, irregardless of the question of service and of this, that, and the other.

Now here is the mental picture.

I start walking east. I'm going to May's. Okay, it is cold out. When I say cold, I mean cold as you-know-what. So why not get a crosstown? Okay, the fare is sixty cents. And this was only a year ago, right? Meaning, I don't have to tell you what the going rate is now! But in my personal opinion, the time could come when the price of bus fare is what stands between you and God-knows-what. Does this make sense to you or does this make sense to you?

Correction: I meant to say *catastrophe* for when I said scandal. I guess you know why. Which is because it was one of the ones of the twenty-three so far. Like this. "Catastrophe." But the thing of it is, I can't tell you which one it went with or whether I heard the click with her which could have been like her contacts.

WAIT A MINUTE. WE WERE TALKING about money.

Here is a perfect example. The knife. Setting aside the fact I am not the type of individual to go in a store and buy one, I wouldn't have, even if I was. You see what I am saying? Paki is going to set up the whole deal for the boy's future. In other words, millions! But would yours truly fork over the few dollars?

Okay, it looks like a contradiction, right? Wrong! Because the contradiction, it makes it just right!

Listen, when I was in the seventh grade, the teacher reads us something. She says this writer is named Walter Whitman, this Walter Whitman from the borough of Brooklyn. I'll be honest with you, the name of the thing I don't remember. But it said something that goes right up at the top of my list with me. It said, "Hey, look at me contradicting myself!"

I love that. Even if it comes out of the same borough as Norman. Look, I won't kid you. No offense to present company, but this Walter Whitman really said something. I mean, this is your real writing in case you missed it.

Let's face it, contradictions, this is the whole story, end of discussion, period!

I say you can say anything. I say if you live long enough, you will! It is all in this thing of contradicting it, isn't it?

Okay, I admit it. This is how Norman got into this in the first place. Put aside the fact he is a famous celebrity. Because the other thing is, he is into this thing of where you can say anything. In other words, he does not knuckle under when it comes to this, that, and the other. He knows that if you can think it, you will do it, and who can't think of everything?

Listen, I have read some of Norman's bestsellers. But you do not have to worry. What Norman knows I say you know double! Just don't make me have to spell it out for you. Some people know this, and some people don't. I am someone who does.

THE POINT IS, I AM WALKING CROSSTOWN when it happens. This is not a neighborhood you are familiar with, okay? So let me fill you in. It is mainly your Spanish, so far as I can see. In other words, your Spanish and your coloreds. Meaning, your dope addicts and so forth. To make a long story short, face facts—it is an unwholesome district.

Now here is the mental picture. On both sides there are

these little shops which are like dribbling out front with all types of merchandise. Meaning, whatever they are selling, they hang it out there to show it to the individuals walking by. So do I have to tell you what the level is of the quality? Add to this the vendors on the sidewalk, which is, for argument's sake, like pushcarts one right next to the other. Long story short, this is how come the foot traffic is almost at a standstill. Actually, this is good. Reason: If something breaks out, it gives you your warning!

Okay. Here is the thing. People make a wave!

This is how it happens. When they do it, what you know is something is definitely coming.

You see what I am saying?

It is like a wave of ocean coming. The second thing is, it always goes in a direction which isn't the one it is supposed to go in. It's like when the ocean goes against the natural nature of things. In other words, watch out, something is definitely coming!

I for one am always set up for this when I am on the streets of Gotham. This is because a decent citizen has to be. Otherwise, here comes bodily harm or worse. So you have to be ready to get out of the way of the wave. You have to look with both eyes! You have to watch for the wrong type of wave!

I say make it second nature.

I don't have to tell you the number of times the boy has been told to do this—make it second nature.

You think I want to scare him? The answer is no. But meanwhile, which is worse, true or false—being jumpy when he has to be, or not being set for the wave when it comes?

I know some people think nine is already old. T.C., for example. She says there are fourth-graders who do things. She says there are fourth-graders who even go take off for school by themselves. I, however, do not think nine years old is old enough. This is my personal analysis. Whereas T.C., she just says, "Lord, Lord."

But I say little boys are here one minute and gone the next. And when they are, I say look to the parents, look to the parents, blame the parents!

Look at the papers, listen to the channels. Let's not kid ourselves, does a day go by where there isn't a child which isn't maimed to death or dismembered? Add to this all the cases you never even hear about because there is too much blood and guts for them to fit it all in.

Take my word for it, the papers and the channels do not have enough room in them for all the terrible things which are going on. One thing you can always count on, the blood and guts is going up like the cost of living. Hey, don't you have to have more and more just for someone to pay any attention? This is why yours truly says what is all the hurry about? Sunday comes, I can see my way clear to maybe letting the boy run down to the corner for the *Times*. But do I let my guard down before he is back where he belongs? Listen, I am in Constant Touch on the seven-watter.

"Red Dog, Red Dog, all clear? This is Blue Dog calling Red Dog, please answer please!"

IN MY HOUSEHOLD, THE TRAINING is my department. I don't have to tell you, where T.C. is concerned, she does not have the patience for it. The thing is why take chances? Let's face it, the wave can come out of anywhere! This is what I am teaching the boy. Which is for him to be all set for it for when it comes, end of discussion, period.

Okay, this is the thing I have mainly noticed, how fast. Bodily harm is the fastest thing which happens. I know. Don't kid yourself, yours truly is the expert.

Which is why you have to watch the foot traffic for the wave. Which is how I am training the boy. I tell him for him to keep his eyes wide open for how the foot traffic is going. You have to keep your eyes peeled for these tiny changes. This is how the wave starts, first this little speeding up here and this little speeding up there, then the next thing you know the whole thing of it is going crazy and is racing in another direction!

Come on, the facts are the facts, this is Gotham! Meaning, you can't act like it is the middle of the Mojave!

All right. I was going to say desert. But I made it Mojave because of the story. I know you wrote it. "Mojave." I read it. I read all your wonderful writing everywhere you write it.

I mean, you can write. In other words, you can write

something and get the money. You just have to have the paper and the pencil. Whereas take me. What can I do? Sure, I used to be on the radio, but where are the programs of today? I don't have to tell you what happened to them! You say, okay, there is your television. But I say this is cameras and everybody looking.

You don't understand. I'll explain later.

No, forget it! What's wrong with right now?

Here is the thing. It is like with the eyes of all of the women. So you say a word, okay? "Impediment," for example. Whereupon whoever it is stares—stops and stares, okay? Are you getting this mental picture?

So far, so good. Meaning, stopping and staring is what happens when you say the word to the women.

"Disdain." There's another, for instance.

So she stops whatever she is doing. Let's just say for argument's sake, you are all of the way at the end of the platform and she is reading the paper.

You're in position. This is the first thing. In other words, the end of the platform and here comes the subway. This way there is the noise. Except not too much of it yet. Hey, check it out! If there is going to be too much of it, can she hear it when you say it?

"Disdain." You can hear this, can't you?

Listen, who's kidding who? The thing of it is, you put your face right up close to hers. I'm talking about just this much away from her face. Hey, a matter of picas, right?

So here come the eyes. Like whatever it is she is reading,

forget it. Because, wait a minute, *disdain?* Somebody said what? Or maybe, for argument's sake, it was *effectuate* or *catastrophe,* just for argument's sake.

So where are we?

The eye, okay?

As to which, you have got your mascara and your eye-liner and your so forth and so on. So meanwhile there is this thing which is the size of the Devil's heel, which is to quote T.C., of course. I mean, it is there in the center part of the colored part. So this is your target.

Bingo!

What I'm saying is, Paki sticks it—the mush, the brain, the eye, the whole business.

So here's another one for the boy and for the question of the future, right? But meanwhile you are forgetting some-thing, which I for one do not blame you doing. Because from when she looks up to when you put Paki in, it's what? Not even a second. But this is long enough for it to be like a television.

Listen, I don't have to tell you!

I mean, do I have to tell you who had a camera? Don't make me have to tell you. Also, who she took a picture of it with and what she did with it when she did.

Don't kid yourself. I found it!

I don't know. Maybe I didn't. Maybe it was where I couldn't miss it.

I have to think about it. Sometimes I think she had it

stuck to the door of the refrigerator. On the other hand, sometimes I don't remember if she did or didn't.

Wait a minute. Here's something. When you do it in the subway, forget about the click. In other words, even if she has on contacts, you think you are going to hear something even if there is something? Tell you what—maybe it always clicks and it's not a question of contacts.

But let's not kid ourselves, what with the circle you are in, this is not your type of transportation, is it?

Am I right or am I right?

I mean, present company on even the Lexington line? Hey, do me a favor and don't make me laugh.

YOU ARE THINKING, OKAY, SO A CAMERA, what's that? It is just an item and who has to look? But I say the thing of it is, you have to. This is because you better! Hey, what if you don't?

It's like just like with the wave. It's the same thing exactly! Meaning, does the wave see you? Hey, forget it. You just happen to be where the wave is going when the wave is going. You see what I am saying? It's like a camera. It gets you caught in it.

Whereas I say it wouldn't if you had shown any sense and stayed on your toes in the corners of your eyes.

I keep telling this to the boy. I say, "Stay on your toes in the corners of your eyes."

T.C. says, "Lord, Lord." She says quit it before I give him

a case of the nerves. I say to her why doesn't she pitch in with the training. But she says, "Let's not and say we did."

I have disdain for the words which go with this subject. Meaning, your words which go with nerves and so on. You say I am saying this is because I was in a place. But it isn't. I guarantee you, this is not the reason.

Whereas the reason is, who can count on them?

Here is an example. When I was in the first one, let's take the thing with the laces. So I don't have to tell you what its name is. But then I'm in the second place. Whereas in the second place they say the name for it is different. You see what I mean? It is the same thing, even the way the sleeves go and even the way they have the laces. Except if you listen to what they say it is, doesn't it kill you it's a camisole?

So you see what they do to you? They say it's a camisole! This is what they say to you even when the sleeves are the same and so are the laces!

God is my judge, this is the situation. They change the words. Take it or leave it, this is what they are doing in the subject I just made mention of. Which is why what can you count on?

Camisole.

Here's another one. Paraldehyde.

TAKE THE CALENDAR. IT HAS a different word for every day. This is so you get a more powerful vocabulary.

Okay, it cost three dollars. But I say it was a solid investment. I say you can't cut corners in this particular department. You see what I am saying? I want the boy to know what's doing when they say something. I do not want him to have to guess as he goes along. This is why a word a day is a step in the right direction. Take the one which comes up after *catastrophe*. Okay, you'll never guess. *Snickersnee!* Can you beat it? It means knife. Hey, live and learn, right?

On the other hand, let's not kid ourselves. I mean, it gets stuck in you, so what's the diff what they come up to you and call it? Am I right or am I right?

Hey, forget it! The thing is, does it hurt? Do you scream from just waiting there waiting for it?

I mean, stop to think, the thing is going in and where it's going and then it's in there in you in all the way. You see what I am getting at? Hey, it's a thing which doesn't belong there. And let's not forget you see it first! You know something? Even if your back is turned, you do.

Check it out. Don't take my word for it. A knife, you do not even have to be looking to know it's on the way. This is why you scream. Meaning, it is because you have to wait. At least this is my personal analysis. In other words, you have to wait to see how much it will hurt. So here is where the scream comes in.

You take the day on Fourteenth Street when yours truly was going to May's. So here are the things—Christmas, the three-speed, save a dollar. These are the things which I am thinking about. When here it comes from where all this merchandise is dribbling from everywhere! Lo and behold, here it comes! It's coming sideways across the sidewalk. You see what I mean about it going in the wrong direction? Hey, it's your wave which is going against the nature of things!

YOU SEE THIS AT THE BEACH.

I saw this at the beach.

I grew up almost on a beach.

The town was even called it—it was called Long Beach. It's the town we moved from house to house in when we moved when I was seven. Remember Buddy Brown? Because that's what Buddy Brown was.

Buddy Brown was a wave.

You know the ocean. You know how the ocean is. Something under it makes it go in the wrong direction. This is when you get the wave. Go figure it. Meanwhile, here it comes—the wave.

Let's face it, I used to see this plenty. Listen, who is the expert in this department? When it comes to oceans, yours truly knows what he is talking about from the word go.

The thing of it is, on account of the ocean I got on the radio. Here's how. I was working on the boardwalk at a certain concession. So next comes Janet R. It is due to her I get on the radio. Okay, to make it one hundred percent, let's just say it is due to Janet Rose's mother's brother, who is, you know, Bill Lido.

But first before Bill Lido there was the wave which came and, you know, took Davie!

HEY, LISTEN, JANET R. IS ALMOST the most important part of everything I am telling you. You'll see—the boy, Janet Rose, my father, these are the things and that's the order of them in the order of their importance. These are the people which are the reason for everything. The rest is just for me to fill you in. I mean like Bobby R. and Davie and my brother's mother, not to mention Buddy Brown and also Ben Bernie.

You know what? This is really something! I mean I never noticed, the two of them, both B.B.! You know what I am doing? I myself am stopping and staring! Hey, and look at this. I don't believe it! T.C. and guess who! Tamara Chris and present company, Mr. Truman Capote!

You see when you stop and stare? You see what starts to happen? Hey, the more you stare at it, the more of it there is there to stare at!

Okay, this reminds me. Fascination! It is the name of the concession I was getting ready to tell you about. This was on the Long Beach boardwalk. Which is where I worked the all-important summer. Which is the summer when yours truly is fifteen. In other words, it's the same summer when Davie gets his medicine. I guess I did not tell you yet the fact that Davie is my brother.

So here is where we are. It is the summer which Davie

has the job of a dancing instructor at one of the hotels on the boardwalk. Whereas yours truly, his job is he is calling color at Fascination.

I am trying to remember the name of the hotel. But I can't and it doesn't matter. The Traymore? Forget it. The thing of it is, Davie is giving lessons in the basement. Sometimes also exhibitions. Granted, he was as good as they come! But not just at dancing. Swimming also. Swimming and dancing, Davie is the expert!

Okay, here are his specialties—the mambo, the rhumba, the samba. It is the summer right around the time the cha-cha-cha is starting to come in. But don't kid yourself, this is another one Davie was already great at!

It goes without saying, I know you like dancing. This is why I make mention to you of the history of these dances.

You take her and my dad, they said they were great ones. They said they danced as a team. I don't know. I never saw it. I only saw it the one time when they said this was what they were doing. But I am willing to go along with the idea that maybe it was back before I was born. The thing of it is, they did not look like the kind of individuals who used to be dancers. Take my dad, he looked like what he was, which is a liquor salesman until he lost his license to operate a vehicle. And so far as she is concerned, she didn't look like anything. All I know is the color her shoes were.

You take the old house, she stayed home. But in the

new one, she went to business. In other words, this is the word she uses. She says, "I am going to business."

But it was like, "I'll only be a minute."

You see what I am saying? It didn't mean what she said it did.

The facts are the facts.

She worked in a store. She took in the money and made change. I mean, if you wanted to find her, you went to the cash register, and this is what she looked like—she looked like a person you didn't look at.

Maybe it was a McCrory's or a Woolworth's or a Kresge's. I don't know. Maybe it was McClellan's. I don't want to remember. Do I have to want to remember?

I think about it. But I don't mind if I don't.

IT'S LIKE WHAT HAPPENED on Fourteenth Street. I think about it. But it's better when I don't. Is this another one of my contradictions?

I don't know. Maybe it is. Maybe it isn't.

Remember when they said what Walter said?

I love that.

It makes everything make sense.

Did I tell you I was in this wave which goes across the sidewalk on Fourteenth? God is my judge, here it comes, whereas not even Christmas and how cold it is could stop it! But who is on his toes in the corners of his eyes, okay? Sure, I am thinking about the three-speed and the money.

But the wave is what I am always thinking about even if I'm not thinking about anything. You have to be crazy not to be ready for it! So say I am a block and a half from May's when it comes at me and gets me in it.

Here is what I was thinking. It's Christmas. I made the walk all of the way over and saved the bus fare. Also, how cold it is. So isn't there bound to be a payoff? Meaning, I will find a ten-speed for the price of a three-speed, with change left over. Look, I figure Christmas, isn't it the job for God to make a miracle?

Okay, so this is the character of my thinking. But don't think I am not also thinking this is one of your worst vicinities. The other thing is the sidewalk. There is all these Spanish and coloreds all over it, not to mention the pushcarts and so on and so forth. You can't move, is the thing! But don't worry, a certain person has his eyes peeled. In times like this I am definitely on my toes in the corners of them in case of the wave which will come before you know it. Forget it, it does not matter that I am thinking about money and a miracle. I'll be honest with you. I am always thinking about money and a miracle. I think about money and a miracle even more than I think about Janet R., and her I think about more than I think about anything except the wave! Correction: I think about you-know-who more than anything in the world.

"Come in, Red Dog—this is Blue Dog, do you copy?"

T.C. says I go overboard in this department. In her personal opinion, the only place which worry gets you is right behind the eight ball. But I say your average person doesn't do it enough! Nobody does. Present company, for example. Hey, are you worried?

Or take me. Was I worried enough when Bill Lido has me up against the wall of the building? Or what about when Janet R.'s mother says I should follow her to the bathroom? Listen, the answer is don't ask.

And doesn't this go double for going into Simon's? Not to mention writing to Mr. M. before I started writing to you.

Notice, I am not even counting leaving Buddy Brown to Davie. But do I really have to? Enough is enough, okay?

Face facts, nobody worries as much as they would if they had the brains to do it! Even I myself don't. And when is yours truly not doing it?

It was so cold. I don't suppose you were in town last Christmas. So how can you know? The television said it was a record. It was freezing even inside. We went to bed with sweaters on and socks. The boy had to wear three pairs of them! Reason: They did not send up much heat up. Meaning, the super and the owners. These winters they send up less and less. But don't think yours truly can't see it from their side of the picture.

Hey, it's murder everywhere. But this is just the start. If it costs you a nickel when you sit down, get ready to fork over a dollar for it by the time you stand up! So meanwhile I was making reference to last Christmas, which let's say you were not here for and instead you were in your Palm Beach or maybe your Palm Springs, which is where I know you always go when the weather is not fit for decent people. So in your case you wouldn't know how cold it was.

No offense, what I said about Palm Springs and Palm Beach. I mean, I realize how it sounds. But I say more power to you! I give you my personal guarantee. Let's face it, you are a famous celebrity bar none! You have given the American public great classics to get where you are. A thousand years from now they will still be singing your praises. Listen, I would be the first one to say you earned it, every nickel. I personally do not begrudge you one red cent of the mountain of money you have. Also, what I said about Palm Springs and Palm Beach. I mean, it might scare you, me knowing where you go when the weather in Gotham is as cold as it was last Christmas. On the other hand, August is also out of the question altogether. This is when your regular people really go nuts—since did they have the smarts to get rich and plan ahead? I don't have to tell you this is what I mean when I say every individual, whoever it is, they can't worry enough! I promise you, if yours truly had done a little more worrying back when, T.C. and the boy could have been right out there with you the day you take off for your place in the Hamptons every August on the dot.

Listen, did I tell you I used to live on the Island too? Okay, I did not live there just for the summer, number one. Whereas number two, I am not saying Long Beach is not a long way from the Hamptons. But you can see the point I mean. On the other hand, the thing of it is, who needed Long Beach once I got to Gotham with Janet Rose and her mother? Hey, this was when I became a definite Gothamite like yourself. True or false, Gotham is our kind of town, meaning present company and yours truly? But look at Norman, right? I mean (joke) Brooklyn, ha ha.

Time out. You think I was mentioning the distance from Long Beach to the Hamptons in miles? Because no way is miles what I was making reference to! Pay attention. It would be very perturbing to me if you started taking me for what Norman did. Meaning, maybe I am not educated, but I know what to measure things in!

I will tell you something I did last week. I measured Paki in picas. Do you know what a pica is? No offense. I was just kidding. Asking you a thing like this is like asking the people in the public if they heard of who I am.

It was my birthday. Forty-seven big ones! So the boy gives me this really thoughtful thing, which is a see-through plastic ruler for true accuracy of measurement! In other words, it has every scale you can think of—including one for measuring in picas.

I thought it was quite a thing for an individual of his age to think of—something wonderful to look at but also something with its practical nature.

Here is something. Paki comes out fifty-two picas with you-know-what when it's out of the handle!

I don't know. Eight and three-quarters still sounds longer to me. But maybe this could be because a pica sounds like something smaller to you, not to mention it really being something which is.

This is a perfect example of why you have to think a thing through. For example, fifty-two is a bigger number than eight is. But the smaller number sounds bigger even if it isn't. But maybe this is because of how we think about knives. Let's face it, so far as yours truly is concerned, this subject is a big mystery, isn't it?

T.C. made her usual, which is the Duncan Hines with cherry icing. Outside of this, that's it and that's it for all the fanfare. I won't kid you, I do not go in for carrying on when it comes to your red-letter days. Too much fooling around and somebody pays the piper in so many dollars and cents. Besides, the more of a big deal you make of it, the more of a fake of it everybody starts making. Add to this how they are already putting on an act in the first place, and you can see how things will get out of hand even before you start going overboard.

Be this as it may, we had an outstanding time irregardless of everything. T.C. and you-know-who sang "Happy Birthday" and then I unwrapped my surprises—the ruler, and the key ring from T.C., which was really a woman in like a telescope with no clothes on. So far, so good. Then we all go out to take in a P.G. afterwards.

Naturally, I do my best in this department. But I do not

have to tell you even your P.G. is going to have parts which are not fit for a certain party. In this day and age, let's not kid ourselves, wherever you turn, something is disgusting! In other words, it is not what it was in our day and age, end of discussion, period.

Listen, I am here to tell you, there was nothing a nine-year-old could not listen to when yours truly was on the radio. Did anybody have to worry about this, that, or the other thing? But forget it. That's definitely bygones. Those days are finished and done with.

Did I tell you I was just a boy myself when I was on the programs? I'll be honest with you, I was on some of the top ones. Go ahead. Check it out. You ask Bobby R. Bobby R. could tell you. Or what about Bill Lido?

I'll give you an example. You name the voice and I could do it. I could sound like anybody, you just name the individual. Okay, you want to hear the payoff? Yours truly could sound like Bobby R. himself!

I promise you, this is no exaggeration. You ask anybody so long as they are somebody who was listening. Meaning, the time he had to take it easy the time on *Young Doctor Malone*. Hey, starring Bobby Readick! But who was really doing it when Bobby R. was vomiting?

Janet Rose, for instance. Didn't she hear just like anybody else? Ask her. She is the individual who could tell you everything I am saying is one hundred percent!

IT WAS SUNDAY. IN OTHER WORDS, the day he rides his bike. Except the Sunday I am talking about is the one that is my birthday. Meaning, T.C. is getting her face on for the P.G., so I am using the see-through to measure things around the house. This is how you give the boy an educational experience. Whereas he could just be waiting for someone to make herself presentable. Just between you, me, and the lamppost, I never miss an opportunity. On the other hand, take my parents. When they saw me listening to the radio, they should have said to me, "All right, here is how it works." And this goes double for the dust and for the vacuum! In other words, it's up to those in the know to tell you! I mean, am I supposed to wait for the radio to tell me how it works? Let's not be ridick!

Okay, the same thing goes for words. Am I right or am I right? This is why the calendar is staying right where it is, whatever T.C. says irregardless! You want to know where I mean? Hint: When a certain person gets up in the morning, it is the first thing he sees. This is because it is on the table and the table is next to his bed!

Listen, I guarantee you, a certain person is never going to have to worry about not knowing how long a minute is.

For your information, it is sixty seconds.

So the next thing is, how long is one of those?

Answer: As long as it takes to get Paki out. And here is how long the next one is.

Long (joke) enough, ha ha.

I DO NOT WANT FOR YOU to get the opinion that yours truly is the kind of individual who does not do something about it when the P.G. gets off-color. Meaning, I have it worked out where yours truly covers a certain person's ears and he himself covers his eyes. I don't have to tell you your average P.G. means it's four times the boy and me are going to have to do this. T.C. says I make mountains out of molehills. But I say T.C. needs to have her head examined, end of discussion, period.

So it's Sunday, and guess what! The word for the day is *absterge*. But meanwhile here is the thing of it. Didn't I just go from the age of forty-six to forty-seven? So this means I have to add one. In other words, long story short, I have to do an extra one the first chance I get. So you see this mental picture? The P.G. is up on the screen and yours truly is sitting there with the page in his pocket when it comes to me like a bolt from the blue I have to do an extra.

Here is when I get up and whisper this. "What say you two to some popcorn or some Good & Plenty?" This is when T.C. goes, "Shush, you, can't you, damn it!" and I go, "I'll only be a minute."

Don't forget it's August. Meaning, who is still in Gotham? Just between us, it's your coloreds and even worse. Meanwhile, this is also why the lobby is more or less empty. But so far as the ladies' room goes, it couldn't be better.

All right.

Are you following me so far in my thinking? Are you

seeing this mental picture? I get out the page in the lobby and I check out the word to be definite. Then I go into the facility to see the situation. Okay, there is one at the mirror and there is one on the toilet. So it goes without saying, I start with the one at the mirror. But do you hear anything in the way of a scream when she sees me? I'll be honest with you, it is all she can do to turn around so Paki is in position.

Listen to this.

"Absterge."

But don't think I don't know I am wasting it on an individual of this level.

In other words, what's the diff, a word which is to these people a foreign language?

Here's something else. Purple lipstick. Also purple where she was putting on more eye shadow on herself until Paki comes along and takes care of business.

Anyway, bingo. But meanwhile I am thinking these three things just to show you my thinking:

Number One) Hurry before more come in.

Number Two) What happens when the one in the toilet hears this one hit the floor?

Number Three) What's the word for the one in there?

Forget it! It all turns out to have no influence one way or the other. Because when I go in under the door of the stall, this particular individual is already out like a light. You know what? She probably heard and keeled over.

All right, I am not going to kid you. So far as yours truly was concerned, even with the eyelid down, I did not see any reason not for me to make the best of it. Meaning, I figure open it up—since for the media you are definitely not thinking straight if you do not stick to your trademark.

Listen, I'll just say this one thing and then I will get back to the original subject. This eye is so bloodshot, who can get a good aim at anything? Another thing is, I have to hold the head up. Enough said? I mean, I am personally no more against anybody than the next one is, but don't make me have to tell you what this colored's hair felt like to me as a person. I promise you, you want to cut your hand off.

Thank God I get back to the seats when I get back to them. This is because, lo and behold, here comes something where as far as I personally am concerned the boy needs to get his hands up over his eyes for, not to mention yours truly has to do ditto over his ears. So while I am doing it, guess what!

T.C. says, "Where is the Good & Plenty? Goddamn it, I'm sitting waiting for the Good & Plenty."

Time out. I just thought of what you are thinking. You are thinking did I take a look the way I did the night it was me which was sitting? Meaning, on the toilet and a certain someone has to shave her legs. Am I right or am I right?

Okay, this is the answer.

No!

First of all, don't forget the factor of taking a powder

before anybody comes. Second of all, the smell, inasmuch as at the time she was doing you-know-what. Third of all, T.C. cannot be trusted. You and I know what to watch for when it comes to your unsuitable material. But does T.C. even have a clue? And even if she did, would she do it? In other words, it could be my birthday, which it was, but would T.C. meet me halfway even for the welfare of the boy?

Forget it!

She would go, "Lord, Lord," and roll her eyes and meanwhile act like it was me who was acting nuts!

Last thing, I promise. But here is something really good. Which is that there is not one peep in the whole theater even by the time the P.G. finishes. Listen, let's face it, your average Gothamite does not want to know from nothing nohow!

Hey, live and let live. Am I right or am I right?

YOU WON'T BELIEVE IT when I tell you how come I remember certain words and don't remember them all. Like *capstone*. I don't really remember that one yet. This is because (joke) so far I haven't used it yet, ha ha.

Camisole. Is this a word I will ever forget? And how about paraldehyde? But I don't have to tell you, you are not going to find them on any calendar, period. Listen, they would not put ones like those on it, I promise you, you don't have to check. On the other hand, you are the wordsmith—so you tell me. How come camisole is the sweatiest word in the world? Or paraldehyde, it's even sweatier. Or pulmotor, there's another sweaty one for you. But here's something—pica and inch. They're sweaty too if you start thinking what they mean.

Hey, I was just thinking—was present company sitting there thinking why does yours truly cover you-know-whose ears? Of course I cover the boy's ears. It could be like on Fourteenth! Or even worse. Meaning, the pizza maker and the man he climbed up on and got up on. Except the real thing is much faster than the thing you see in the movies. But this is not the only thing which makes the real thing different. There are these other things. You have to see. You have to hear. I did. I saw it on Fourteenth. In other words, I saw the one who was afraid the most was the one who had the knife. Four boys, but who's afraid the most? Forget it. It's dancing. They move. It's like sleepy people dancing in the goo they are sticking in dancing in. This is what it's like—fast things going slow because you look and see them in their parts. It is different than anything else. It looks gooey. But it isn't. It is in a class by itself. You know what it is? It is bodies moving how they never had to. That's it! It looks gooey-looking. But this is because you are looking!

I did and didn't look. It was freezing. There was ice. Add to this the wind. Oh, all the things I heard!

Personally, I do not like it when this is how cold it gets. Ice is another thing. Ice is even worse. I'll be honest with you, when people fight, ice is the worst thing they can fight on. Okay, this is only one man's theory, but my theory is ice makes everything as bad as anything can get.

Here is the mental picture.

One of the boys slips.

Which one? Guess!

I call them boys, okay? But let's just say who knows exactly. Maybe the twenties, maybe the teens. Granted, when it comes to your Spanish, yours truly is no expert.

I am forty-seven. Didn't I tell you I had a birthday? Most people in the public wouldn't say so. Most people in the public would say thirty-five, give or take. First of all, I have not lost my looks. I am very nice-looking. I was very nice-looking. I guarantee you, when Janet R. passed a remark to the contrary, I for one could tell what she was up to. Okay, looks. So what do you think Buddy Brown looks like in this day and age? I promise you, nobody's mother is taking any Buddy Brown's picture for the fridge now!

All right, so looks are more or less the thing. You think I don't know this theory will not fall on deaf ears so far as present company is concerned? Even after we moved, people made over me. I still had my looks when I turned eight. I was still a picture-book boy. Let's face it, to this very day, people still stop and stare. Not that I spend big bucks on it. Far from it. Listen, what they get for just a normal haircut nowadays, I don't have to tell you. Whereas if you want a little style to it, forget it! Am I right or am I right? I mean, you could buy a new head for what they quote you for a haircut in the world of today. You know what? I could write a book about what they're doing to the price of things. Let's not kid ourselves, you get haircuts. You know what the score is. It's time somebody said something, enough said? I'll be absolutely honest with you, back in our day and age you could get a ten-speed for what a haircut of today is going for in a decent location!

Okay, an actor has to watch his hair. On the other hand, I don't see an individual laying out that kind of money if all you are is on the radio. They can't see you on the radio. It's like a writer's hair, okay? I mean, who sees the hair of a writer when a writer is sitting down with their pencil and their paper writing their bestsellers?

On the other hand, there is the picture on the cover of your bestsellers. Whereas I am just in Payroll in my branch, when all is said and done.

You see what happens when I don't go slow enough and think a thing through?

BILL LIDO HAD SUCH TERRIFIC HAIR ON HIM, curly and brown. Janet Rose had the same kind. T.C.'s got this almost white hair, whereas Sylvia Berman's was long and black and came straight down. Meanwhile, Buddy Brown had the greatest hair you ever saw—blond and like the light was in it all of the time. Here's something. It's the kind of hair a mother uses her own hairbrush on.

Come on, I was not born yesterday. Meaning, looks are

definitely the thing. Listen, if I didn't have them, you think they would have had me calling color? I'm talking about at Fascination—you think they would? That summer or any other? Hey, do me a favor and don't make me laugh.

But who am I to tell you?

You think I don't know about the pictures of yourself you put on your bestsellers?

It is what the people in the public notice. Hey, you are not just another wordsmith with a collegiate education! Forget it. They are a dime a dozen. You are a wordsmith who looks like a million bucks!

This is how it was with yours truly. In other words, I wasn't just a good boy—I was a good boy who also looked like that. I'm telling you, everything loved me for it. I was loved. I was watched. In a manner of speaking, everything was taking pictures of me. You see what I am saying? The sky was taking pictures of me. So big deal if she didn't! Big deal if it would have broken her arm for her to get out her camera for anybody but Buddy Brown!

The thing of it is, it was a feeling I had. You see what it was? The feeling was what it was I moved in when I moved! I mean, the same way you move, except for me it was different. Or in the water if you're in this instead.

Naturally, there is nothing I have greater disdain for than the disdain I have for being photographed. I mean, name me the camera that's fair! You see the thing I'm getting at? Let's say there was a camera which could really do it, be fair. So if there was, then you'd have how many brands in the business? Does this make sense or does this make sense? Hey, it's like I told you, yours truly was definitely not born yesterday!

Radio was a different proposition altogether. There was the microphone. You talked into the microphone. It did not look back at you and take a picture of you when you weren't ready. It didn't measure you in so many picas. It didn't say it took so many of you to make one Buddy Brown!

FORGET ACTING. FORGET RADIO. That's bygones, that's ancient history, that's water under the proverbial bridge. In other words, I work in a bank. This is where I found Paki. I think I already told you—meaning, in Payroll, right?

Another thing, it is one of your top ten in Gotham, this establishment. According to the figures which come out, this is where it is in the figures. Up there in the top ten, end of discussion, period.

We're Midtown. Let's just say East Side in the lower Fifties. This means I can make it over to Peartree's on the lunchbreak. Whereas for you from your place, it's what? A block, right? I mean, your apartment, it is how far from Peartree's or from there to Antolotti's? Okay, for you it is a matter of let's say convenience. In other words, face facts, what they put on a plate at your P.'s and your A.'s is not exactly what they put on a plate at your Cote Basque!

Believe me, I am not saying it is my custom to dine at this level. Listen, it's no secret. I mean, even P.'s is out of the ballpark for yours truly. I'm talking, of course, about your full-dress three-course, soup to proverbial nuts. But I don't have to tell you, your French cuisine these are definitely not! Naturally, with me it is all in my imagination, okay? I am making reference to the true nature of the cuisine of this type. But Cote Basque, what say we give it a tumble when present company and yours truly sit down together to break bread together and finalize our business? Hey, I won't kid you, when it comes to French, count me in. I mean, I'm no expert, but I wouldn't mind taking lessons!

THERE I GO. IT WAS THE MENTAL PICTURE. Meaning, Janet Rose and how she liked to French. It gives me the mental picture of Germaning or of Jewishing or of something along these lines. T.C., for example. Maybe this is what she wants, Saleming or Oregoning. I don't know. It is just that when it comes to French, T.C. says forget it!

Don't kid yourself, Frenching was what Janet Rose was great at. But the next thing you know, she got sidetracked. Let's just say I have in mind the hairbrush.

Face it, up until the change in her, it was my privates which got the attention. Listen to this. One time we squished it back and forth. Do you see the mental picture? From her to me and from me to her and so on and so forth. Lo and behold, before you know it, your jizz is all gone from these little different swallows of it.

I wish T.C. would stop to think of something for her to do along these lines.

Hey, you think this subject is off-color?

Believe me, it is not my nature to make mention of things which are things which are off-color. Far from it. I am sorry if I just said something which lowers myself in your eyes. But here is the reason. You need to have the mental picture. This was another mistake I made with the famous celebrity who lives in Brooklyn. In other words, I did not let my hair down with him, and maybe he could tell it. Whereas with you, I know I can put my feet up and make myself at home.

But present company can see this, can't he? I mean, you can see how with you it's not like it was with Norman.

Okay, I guess you caught me. It's the truth. I'm still a little jumpy. And here is something else where I wasn't one hundred percent aboveboard with you.

It is about Fourteenth, isn't it? I mean, I made a certain statement. I said I don't go down there as a habit, but I was fibbing, take it or leave it. First of all, it's the buys on all the staples. So number one, I admit it, it's the savings.

Whereas number two, it's the spot where it happened. Not that there is anything to see anymore. But this is the thing which interests me. Let's face it, even the next day there wasn't.

This is nothing new in Gotham, blood and guts all over

the place one day and no blood and guts anywhere the day after that. Meaning, it's just back to all the filth it was in the first place. People don't care what they step in. Your foot traffic wears everything off. Hey, you name it! Only just only one only head, but you can't believe what came out of it! On the other hand, this was the one exception. But it goes without saying that an individual fat as her, you had to expect it to be different. God is my judge, you should have seen it!

I don't know. Maybe Paki touched a kind of clot in there or cyst or something. Or maybe there was some kind of infection. The thing of it is, it kept on bubbling out like it is something which has this like gas in it.

You know what? I say your average Gothamite would come along and not give it a second thought. You see my line of reasoning? Live and learn. But I am here to tell you, these individuals will step in anything!

So long story short, Fourteenth was just like nothing ever happened. Whereas suppose the same amount of you-know-what was on the sidewalk out there where all of the famous celebrities are out there in the Hamptons. So say you come back the day after to take a look at it. Hey, you would really see something, true or false?

But maybe I am just kidding myself. Maybe they just go ahead and walk on everything everywhere.

I don't know. If it happened on ice, it wouldn't last no matter where it was. Another thing, maybe there are no sidewalks in the Hamptons. But you tell me. Isn't this the way it is where the houses are really nice? No sidewalks, just the nice road with the nice limos on it?

Like I told you, I am from the Island myself. Not that present company really is—or even that you are a real Gothamite. New Orleans, right? Hey, I know what the story is. It's no secret. Listen, I grew up somewhere different myself. Who didn't? T.C., for example. She is from Salem, Oregon. You see what I mean? In a manner of speaking, nobody isn't from somewhere else. Look at my dad. Or Janet R. They are not even where you could say they are even anywhere anymore!

Hey, from New Orleans to Gotham to your private table at the Cote Basque! You name me the individual, and yours truly will only be too glad to take his hat off to them if they can point to something like that!

Much as they like to act big, I do not think the bank officers that come into my zone have ever actually eaten there. Meaning, the C.B., of course. Antolotti's is more their speed. But I am not saying these are your top men. So far as I can see, the top ones you don't know about because they don't come around and show up in Payroll.

I would make mention of their names for the record. But I do not see why I have to involve my employer in my time off when I am at home. But listen to this. Present company passes by this branch. You pass it. It is on the way. I mean, chances are your limo has to when you go to eat your French cuisine at you-know-where.

It was new seven years ago. But I don't have to tell you how run-down it is now. When I first moved into it from a different one, it made me proud to be in this one. But now this is water over the dam. It is ridick, I know, but when a place you're in runs down, you think you did it too. On the other hand, this is Gotham—so isn't this where your wear and tear come from? You give it seven years in Gotham, nothing is going to look like new to you, not even a branch of one of your top-ten banks.

A WRITER WOULD NOT KNOW what I am talking about. A writer does not have a building. Your writer is more like your actor, page here, page there—Gotham, the Hamptons, Palm Beach, Palm Springs—never the same situation for themselves day in and day out.

Granted, this is only your top people. You and Norman, for example. Whereas your others, they probably do their writing all in one place. But let's face it, wherever they're doing it, it's not like sitting in Payroll year in and year out.

Listen, let's not forget this. When I was on the radio, it was different. I was in a studio! Or take Bobby R., for instance, so long as we're talking about your top individuals. He used to do what? Eight shows on a good day? Not that we called them shows in that day and age. We called them programs, this was your professional term. God is my judge, Bobby R. was making good money. Fifteen minutes here, fifteen minutes there, time out for commercial announcements. I wonder how much he did. Ann Shepherd too. Don't kid yourself, she must have cleaned up. Well, let us just say it was, you know, Scheindel Kalish (joke) who did, ha ha.

You remember Mutual—the Mutual Broadcasting System? Remember when they used to say, *This is Mutual, the world's largest network.* Or sometimes, *This is radio for all America, the Mutual Broadcasting System.* This is what Bill Lido said. No kidding, he did.

I did all my programs on Mutual. I'll be honest with you, this is where Bill Lido worked.

Believe me, I was once next to the big money once. But let's not kid ourselves, it was peanuts alongside what present company and the boy are going to take in on the book of my life and my death. Am I right or am I right?

Hey, I just thought of this. At the bank, I am next to the big money day in and day out so long as you don't count (joke) weekends and holidays, ha ha.

I have been with this organization seventeen years. I have the highest respect for my colleagues—in this branch and in all of the others. But it is not the same as it used to be. Everything is different now. Did I tell you the building is getting run-down? I think I did, but I don't have the time to go back and check it out.

On the other hand, nothing is so high and mighty it can't come down a peg or two, bank buildings included. Maybe even all the pegs there are. Picas and inches and pegs. Just wait and it will.

Here is a funny mental picture. How many pegs are you? Who is more pegs, you or Norman? Or let's say between the man who made pizzas and the other one in the sport coat, where are the pegs in this situation? In your personal theory, what do you think, one so tall and one so short? Or is it supposed to be vice versa?

You take the people which frequent the Cote Basque. I mean, the people in that circle. Don't they have to walk the sidewalks just like everybody else? Do you see what I'm saying? Nobody can stay off the sidewalk even if they try. So let's say you are on it. Can't it come at you when you are?

This is why you have to stay on your toes in the corners of your eyes, end of discussion, period.

A person could be walking out of a place. For instance, out of, let's say, the Cote Basque. He could be thinking of his new bestseller. He could be thinking how the money is coming in when the wave comes in instead. Take me. I mean, this is how it was last Christmas. I was thinking about the money just the way you could have been. Hey, I am always thinking about it, just between us fellows.

Tell me the truth. Do you make reference to it as the Cote Basque or the C.B.?

You have to get a mental picture of this to believe it. Four youngsters, one with a knife. But meanwhile the one cutting is also the one which is scared! Let's not kid ourselves, this was something to see. I am tall enough. In other words, I can follow the action. Besides, the foot traffic is mainly your Spanish, give or take the same exceptions. In this situation, five-nine to five-eleven is tall enough, okay?

So the wave comes, and it carries me into the middle of the street. The next thing you know, the wave starts going the other way. This is because they're pushing back to see. It is also because of the three of them which are trying to get away. Meaning, get away from the one with the knife! Do you follow this mental picture? They don't want them to! Meaning, it doesn't—it being the wave which switches and starts going back the other way.

Here is something I do not have to spell out for you. Which is that with Paki, it's different. Notice, I am not saying this is how it is always going to be. In other words, we are talking about what? Only twenty-three individuals so far? So who knows with the twenty-fourth?

But meanwhile, here is my theory for what it's worth. Just don't put this in the book unless in your personal opinion it checks out for you one hundred percent!

Okay, the thing of it is is this. Let's just say for the sake of argument there are people behind the one I'm going to say the word to, or there are people behind yours truly. You see this mental picture? Granted, there never was to date—but we are just talking for argument's sake.

The question is, do you think if this was the case, pushing would come into it?

My answer to you is a definite no.

Here's why. One push and that's it!

At least, this is my opinion personally. Meaning, right in front of her you-know-what.

You see what I am saying? Because with Paki, it is a question of, let's not kid ourselves, of picas.

People in the public want to see. But so far as pushing goes, do they or don't they? I have to stick to my theory and say the answer is a definite answer of no!

But this is the best I can do as per the particulars. In other words, it's guesswork. Granted, I am in a position to speak as an expert. But even so, I'm talking to you only as a layman, if you see what I mean.

Listen, I'll be honest with you. I say you will have to go to the books on the subject if you are looking for the reason behind the reason. Or maybe you know a professional individual who specializes in this department. Do what your heart tells you. This is the best policy. I just want to get you thinking in the right direction.

SO GETTING BACK TO THE PEOPLE on Fourteenth, even if the wave pushed, it didn't have to. This is because the boys wanted to go. Granted, they were cut. I mean, just look at the blood to begin with. But even so, the boys which are bleeding didn't need any pushing. The thing of it is, far from it. Meaning, they weren't the ones which were scared. Whereas the scared one was the one which was cutting! So is this crazy or is this crazy?

Here's something. The shirts is where you see it when you see the blood. On the ice you couldn't.

Here is something else—white shirts. As God is my witness, just shirts, white shirts, no sweaters, no coats, no jackets! Notice, cold as bad as this, but just shirts, all four of the boys which are getting cut and cutting.

I just had a theory. Okay, I have not made a special study of this, but maybe it is a Spanish thing. In other words, that element, maybe white shirts is what they wear when, you know, it's Saturday or Christmas.

The thing of it is, the tails are out. Another thing is, they flop around like they are floppy because they are wet with something. I don't think it's just the blood. Here is my thinking. The cold was what it was!

So what do you think? You think the cold can make you get floppy like that? Maybe it is some kind of current which goes through the air when the air is cold enough. Like what if the dust gets frozen, so things get like that?

But to make a long story short, it's a thing you can't forget. Also the screaming—the way it does not sound like boys but dogs screaming. That's it! Dogs screaming. Like you stepped on their foot and they are screaming from it and screaming.

Here is something else. It's all of them! It's not just the ones which are cut but also the one which is cutting. Hey, you really have to hear it with your own two ears because I can't give you the mental picture of it. God is my judge, if you did not hear it, you would not believe it.

Okay, you go to the movies, but I say forget it! As far as I am concerned, the movies are all wet from the word go.

This goes double for the channels which T.C. watches. You see what I'm saying? It's dogs screaming and shirts looking floppy-looking. You think they could handle a thing like this on the channels or in the movies? Don't kid yourself, they couldn't. They wouldn't get to first base.

I saw it. There is no comparison. For example, the one with the knife, his arm was like this. Stiff, even when he's cutting, it's stiff. So what is your opinion of this? You think maybe the cold or the fear froze it?

Hey, I made that up. Okay, I was just kidding. It was just an icebreaker. Forget it. I was just breaking the ice because things were getting too serious.

But this is something solid. This you can put in the book. The knife, I never saw it! I'm all eyes, but where is it? Face facts, you know where it is, but you don't see it!

ON THE OTHER HAND, WHEN I FOUND PAKI you-know-where, you couldn't miss it. So how come nobody saw it before yours truly? In the final analysis, this is not the kind of an item an individual could look at and not know they are seeing it. So it makes you think, doesn't it? Meaning, is Paki waiting for a certain someone to see it? Does this make sense or does this make sense?

Get this. There is brass on both ends of the handle, whereas there are steel rivets in the wood part. A lot of big rivets on one side, a lot of big rivets on the other. The thing of it is, they curve in the curve which the handle goes in. But maybe you call them grommets. I don't know. The important thing is, they make Paki look bigger. So how could anyone miss it when the thing of it is it is sitting right there on the copier?

I didn't.

I took one look and guess what? I saw it.

Here is the mental picture. There is this little room right next to Payroll. Which is the room that's just for the copier. So this is where Paki is—right on top of the copier!

Time out. Granted, it is telling tales out of school, but the point is it goes to show you. It's what T.C. says when she makes mention of the Xerox they have in the office she goes to. Like this—Exrox. She goes, "Lord, Lord, I am sick to death of always having to Exrox everything."

You see what I am saying? This is what happens when you watch the wrong channels. Let's face it, her and her *Charlie's Angels*. Which is guess whose favorite program.

Okay, I for one am not pointing a finger. Meaning, it makes you laugh, granted. But we all have to have something. You name me the individual, and yours truly will show you where there's always something, take it or leave it.

Take me, for example. Let's say I get a call from Nature and have to you-know-what. So just for argument's sake, let's just say. Whereas the thing of it is, you'd think I'd do it standing up, but yours truly doesn't!

You see what I mean when I say everybody has something? But when you stop to think about it, what's the reason? Because the thing of it is, there is always a reason. Okay, yours truly sits. Except what is the reason?

Here is the reason. If you sit, then between you, me, and the lamppost, can anybody hear you when I do it?

So now you know. But you say, okay, what if no one is there for them to listen? The answer to this one is easy. Which is that I am, end of discussion, period.

Don't kid yourself. You can live and learn when it comes to how someone like yours truly feels about their feelings! Believe me, I have plenty of them!

TIME IN AGAIN.

So there's Paki. In other words, the copier is what Paki is right on top of. This is why I ask you why am I the first one to spot it? On the other hand, maybe it is, you know, Paki which spots me. Okay, forget it! I guess it sounds to you like I have got a screw loose. The thing of it is, I was only proposing a theory.

Hey, here I am sitting here thinking you go into the Cote Basque and it's no different. So let's just say you go into the famous restaurant which present company frequents. So you go in there. And you know what you see? I say you don't see anything until it's ready for you to see it!

Okay, so you tell me. Am I right or am I right? I mean, there it is, and it's fabulous, but what about this and that in particular? Granted, I am not in a position to say one way or the other, am I? But my guess is you see so much you don't see anything! Listen, do you think you would see a knife? Even if it was probably a knife which was where you didn't expect it?

So the same thing goes for the copier room next to Payroll. This is why it makes you think. Okay, here is the thought in words of one syllable. What is the reason nobody sees Paki until along comes yours truly? To tell the truth, I would like to hear your personal opinion.

On the other hand, go stand at the door of where I and mine live. You see the difference? Sure, the whole thing comes from stores you don't want to shop in. But do you see all of the crap at once? The answer is a definite no. Take my word for it, it is one piece of crap at a time!

But getting back to where I was, I have to take a big deep breath first. I really have to. In other words, I am sitting here trying to get myself calm and collected.

Okay, so I see Paki, and the first thing I think is Simon's. Then I think, "This is a knife but who does this knife belong to?" So here is how I answer. The repairman! I say to myself, "The repairman must have been here and went away and forgot it!"

Here is something else I think. Maybe there is a spot in the copier and the repairman has to touch it. Whereas the only way you can do it is with the knife. You see what I am saying? Okay, it is crazy, but this is the thought which comes to me. Which is that even a thing like the copier has a you-know-what! In other words, it is like with the opposite gender and there is this little special little spot inside of it. So the man has to come along and be there when they call him and this then, this knife, this is how he touches it.

Let's face it, it makes you stop and think. Meaning, maybe with everything there is there is a place like this and you have to reach in with something to get to it. But, okay, this is just a thought I have. I mean, don't think I really think a copier can actually have one! First of all, why would it? Second of all, a thing like a Devil's heel, what would be the reason behind it? On the other hand, you never know, do you? Listen, I'll be honest with you. Even if it is a crackpot theory, it couldn't hurt to check it out. Except forget it!—I mean, who's kidding who? Believe me, would anybody ever tell you!

I DON'T KNOW. YOU SIT HERE and everything makes you stop and think. On the other hand, who am I to tell you about a thing like this? Because who is the expert? But for what it's worth, I'll just go ahead and tell you what I just thought. Which is that with food it's no different!

Tell me I'm crazy, but I say the facts are the facts. Meaning, you swallow something and what do you say? You say it hits the spot or you say it doesn't. Does this make sense or does this make sense? Because it makes sense.

Hey, here's something. When I was the age the boy is now, everything hit it and the same goes for Davie. Don't kid yourself, we were hungry. But this is as far as it goes.

Meaning, in all of the other departments, Davie was one thing and yours truly was another!

Talk about things we were good at, for instance. With Davie it was swimming and dancing, whereas with yours truly I don't have to repeat myself. You name it, it was voices of every description!

You know what? This is something else I never thought of. I mean, there I am on the radio with one of my millions of voices, whereas out in the audience there is a little boy just like I was! You see what I am saying? In other words, his parents didn't tell him either. So what does he think? The answer is the same thing I did! Meaning, the radio! I mean, he thought I was in it instead of on it!

Hey, believe me, I am not pointing a finger. Far from it! Let's not kid ourselves, when it came to listening to the radio, I always did it. Let's face it, they were all my favorites. *Young Doctor Malone*, you take that one—we used to listen to that one together. Up until the time she went to business, that's the one we always used to listen to together. I mean, see if you can see the mental picture. I'm on the hassock and she's in the chair and the light is coming in from behind her. Whereas the other things are the needle and thread and *Young Doctor Malone* on the radio!

Except this was back before I was on it. You ask Bill Lido if I wasn't. He's the one which got me on it. It's just that it's too complicated to explain to a beginner. Face facts, it would be like present company trying to tell yours truly about how he writes his bestsellers. True or false, it takes your expert to spot your expert and vice versa!

Bobby Readick, he could get the Nobel Prize in Breathing. If they give a prize for it, he should get it. Because the whole thing of it is how you breathe. You take Bobby R. when he was Doctor Malone. Believe me, this was breathing bar none! Except here's the thing. When it came to breathing, I was the second best there was.

But it's all a question of nobody seeing you when you do it. Whereas take television, the answer is they do.

Let's face it, breathing is a subject by itself. The word *because,* for example. Or the word *with.* You know what Bobby R. could get out of a word like that? Hey, I don't have to tell you! Listen, name me a writer who can do a thing like this, present company excluded!

You think Norman could?

Hey, don't make me die laughing.

I'm telling you what Bobby R. deserved. The Nobel Prize for Breathing! Ask anyone. Ask Scheindel Kalish— only don't forget the name to look for her by.

I don't do voices in this day and age. There is no call for it in Payroll. "Calling Doctor Malone, calling Doctor Malone, calling Doctor Malone!"

I was just kidding. That was just an icebreaker. I know what a bank is. Or a minute, ask me about a minute.

Hey, live and learn. Enough said?

ACTORS ARE THE WORST, always making jokes, always thinking so much of themselves. But I say writers are probably no different. I bet you know some it would make a person sick to talk to. Look at the pictures some of them pick. I mean, the pictures they pick for some of their bestsellers. Hey, some of them, you can see it sticking out all over them, always thinking of themselves and never ever of not even of anybody else!

It's the same thing with your rich people. In my analysis, there are rich people which make you want to vomit. This is why I should get down on my hands and knees and thank you for writing that story. Hey, you know the one. About the rich people when they're all eating at the fabulous C.B.?

God is my judge, you really gave it to them good! But I say they had it coming. Listen, when a person has it coming, then a person has it coming. Whereas here comes present company and really gives it to them in the chops!

"La Cote Basque." Wasn't that what you called it? What a title! It says a mouthful. Watch out! Here it comes! It's just a person writing, but it's the wave, run for your lives!

I was just wondering. You think I could use it instead of one of them from the calendar? How about instead of *capstone?* "La Cote Basque." So what do you think? You think it would work? You think she would say to herself, "He said what?" You think it would open up her eyes?

No kidding, the people you went after in there—hey, they didn't see it coming, but it came! Wham! It was fast.

In other words, it was like you yourself were the fellows in Kansas. Hey, you know the ones I mean! Wasn't it you which made them famous? You wrote the book on it, true or false? Let's put it this way. Here they come and everybody gets it. Wham! The whole family, okay? But the thing is that nobody really got it last Christmas. I mean, when the wave came when yours truly was on the way to check out May's.

It was just cutting, but I say this made it worse. Now here's the worst thing of it. The boys getting cut keep going back to get cut some more. Do you see what I'm saying? Is this the worst or is this the worst? Listen, I was there. I heard. It was on the ice, but I heard. I mean like dogs, like little dogs. And the knife! You know where it is, but can you see it? Maybe this is the reason. I mean, maybe they can't either! Hey, you think they didn't even know what was making them bleed?

I don't know. It made me sleepy just to watch. It was like with Ben Bernie back in my day and age. It was like with Ben Bernie coming on and going off and giving you his wonderful sign-off.

YOU KNOW WHAT ELSE I HEARD? Someone's yelling "Fight! Fight!" But you can't tell if it means here's one or do it. On the other hand, the paper when they threw it, this was the worst thing of all. I mean, the boys which are cut keep picking things up. They pick up these pieces of things on the ice. In other words, whatever the trash is in the vicinity of this particular caliber. Do you see this mental picture? They pick it up and they throw it! These are the things when they did it. Matchbooks and newspaper and shoppings bags! Which is why it's the worst thing of everything of all. I mean, paper, right? What they're throwing is paper at the boy who has the knife!

Okay, I will be honest with you. Here is another thing we better get straightened out. But it wasn't that I didn't mean to be aboveboard. It was only because when I am going so fast, the next thing I know is yours truly gets all balled up. This is why right at the outset we should have had more time-out for big deep breaths to get less sweaty. Am I right or am I right?

Okay. It's not the *Times* we send him out for Sunday morning. It's the *News*. Enough said?

Let's face it, I didn't want to lower myself in your eyes, end of discussion, period. Is this human nature or is this human nature? But it is not something yours truly is going to sit here and be ashamed of. So we get the *News*. But the thing of it is, it's only because of the money.

I mean, big deal, so Sunday we get the Sunday *News*, whereas for the *Times* they quote you a quarter additional. Okay, maybe I am just in Payroll and maybe I haven't partaken yet of the cuisine at Peartree's yet, but does this mean yours truly has to make his apologies for a slip of the tongue back when my mind was on something else?

Forget it. Let's let bygones be bygones! The thing is, I am doing my best to let my hair down.

Listen, don't think I take any chances when T.C. sends him out to get it. The bike for last Christmas you already heard about. But way before that I really spent the big bucks. Didn't I already tell you? The walkie-talkies? The seven-watters? Let's face it, you know what kind of range this gets you? So if he goes to the corner to pick up the paper, who's with him every step of the way?

"Red Dog, Red Dog, this is Blue Dog checking in."

Certain persons say this is going overboard, certain persons being a certain somebody's ball and chain. But I say you can't be too careful. You take the question of bodily harm, let's not kid ourselves, okay?

"Red Dog, Red Dog, this is Blue Dog calling Red Dog! Answer, please!"

You see what I mean? So say he goes down to the corner to pick up the paper. So even if he went a block out of his way! Hey, come on. Seven watts? Seven watts, you're talking range! I mean, where he couldn't hear me from is a place that's not even on the map! It's like with the vacuum, all that noise, but I can hear it going *Davie, Davie, Davie, Davie.* You see what I am saying? You don't even have to be listening, but you hear it over the noise. Or in the noise. I don't know. Ask her. She is the one that made it run!

The difference is, he hears it from his pocket. In other words, there's all the difference. So the thing is, it's just the opposite. *Davie, Davie, Davie,* it makes you a little sweaty for you to hear it. But when the boy hears yours truly coming in from his pocket to him, it's like everything's all okay, isn't it?

So you tell me. Around the C.B., what kind of voices is it? You know what my theory is? I'm just guessing, but I'll bet some of the old greats go in there. Bobby R. and Bill Lido. Hey, how about Ben Bernie? Let's face it, these are your top names. They are the boys with the big bucks, not to mention you yourself and our fine-feathered friend in Brooklyn.

"Good day, Mr. Capote. What a delight to see you with us again, Mr. Capote."

"Thank you, André, I am thrilled to be back."

"Will you be lunching alone, Mr. Capote?"

"Yes, thank you, André—I shall be alone today."

"Very good, Mr. Capote. And how is your new bestseller? I trust it is selling well."

"Just grand, thank you, André. If you tune in to Johnny tonight, you shall hear me talking about my new bestseller."

"Thank you, Mr. Capote. It will be a delight to tune in to Johnny tonight. Please enjoy your eats with us."

Will you just listen to me! I could probably be a famous celebrity as a writer myself if I really stopped and put my mind to it. Hey, don't kid yourself. I mean, I know there are professional secrets. Like maybe the Word-a-Day calendar is one of them right there! Just between you, me, and the lamppost, true or false? Be honest with me, is it? Hey, are you kidding, you think I can't keep a secret?

You should have heard me on the radio. I don't know, maybe you did. You probably heard me the time I was Young Doctor Malone. Sure, Bobby R. was great, I grant you. But what do you think yours truly wouldn't have ended up being if things had been different?

On the other hand, nobody called color better than I did. Meaning, when I did it at Fascination. Naturally, I am making reference to the all-important summer. But to make a long story short, I better start at the beginning.

It was your top concession.

HERE IS THE MENTAL PICTURE.

There's this place which is open at one end, which is where the boardwalk goes past it. So the people walk along the boardwalk, and there are all of these concessions which come one right after another. Here are some examples— ringtoss, penny toss, cork poppers, rod and reel. So there are all of these choices, right? I mean, I gave you some of them, but those weren't even the half of it!

Okay, so let's say you run ringtoss. Meaning, the people in the public go by, but you don't want them to go by ringtoss and go to penny toss, do you? So this is where you calling color comes in. In other words, somebody has to do it. Which at Fascination is yours truly. At Fascination yours truly is the one which calls the color.

Listen, I'll be honest with you. Up until now I was thinking about giving present company a little demonstration. You know, "Roll the ball, roll the ball, don't hold the ball, don't hold the ball, roll it slow and roll it steady, steady and get ready!" But let's face it, I'm out of practice. So you will just have to use your imagination. Because to my way of thinking, it is a far, far better thing if I do not give you the wrong impression. But for what it's worth, they didn't come any better.

The thing is, it was good money. Whereas this was the summer when we really started needing it. Here's why. They took his license away. Something happened. My dad, I mean. Something happened, and they did it!

She was still bringing in something. You know, she had her position at McClellan's or wherever. But my dad, it was different. I was fifteen, but I could see things were in a situation. I mean, the man has to get around to sell his liquor, doesn't he? So what is the man going to do, take a train?

He didn't take anything. He just went to bed and then he went away. You heard me. Away. That's it.

Hey, we had this house full of samples. I won't kid you. We had your full selection of alcoholic beverage. You name it, we had it! But the truth of it is, in my house we didn't use it. Maybe a little sherry on a red-letter day. Except you can count me out. I mean, even when it comes to your special occasion, skip it, I don't touch the stuff.

Hey, ask Gary. Believe me, you can go ahead and ask

him, it's a free country. You ask Gary if that man has ever seen me touch it—and I mean even once!

Yours is pink peppered vodka. I mean, that's your drink, fair enough? Hey, I know some things. Listen, let's be honest with each other. How does it make you feel knowing yours truly knows an inside thing like this?

Personally, I don't figure it. I mean, how do you swallow the stuff? Pink liquor with pepper in it, don't kid yourself, I'm sorry, but this is one for the books!

You know something? Janet R.'s mother! Hey, was she a thirsty individual or was she a thirsty individual? You know what I say? I say not even Gary himself ever saw anybody thirsty as that! It's scary, isn't it?

Wait a minute. Time out! I just remembered. Okay, the facts are the facts. But I promise you, I'm not hiding anything. Granted, I came close once, but you ask Gary if I ever really did it. I mean it, be my guest. You ask Gary next time you see him. He'll tell you how close I came. But when it got down to actually giving him my order, I changed my mind at the last minute. God is my judge. Hey, you go into Peartree's and see if they don't tell you!

I guess I don't have to tell you when it almost happened. In other words, it was right after the pigeon-toed one, she being the one I first used Paki on. Meaning, I'm on my lunchbreak with time left over after I do her. Whereas Forty-ninth and First is right around the corner!

To tell you the truth, I think I could have used something with a little more kick to it. So I am standing there and I am saying to myself, "Here comes Gary, get ready to place your order." I mean, the man comes and asks me, and I say, "Make mine the usual." Granted, I came close. But when the time came, I said, "Make mine the usual."

Let's face it, it's the old story—the liquor salesman's son and so forth and so on.

This will interest you. I mean, how it went the first time.

Number one, I'm going to get my egg roll. Now when it comes to egg roll, you never know what you're getting. This is why you have to know who you're giving your business to. Because you're crazy if it's just anybody. So walking distance from the branch, we're talking about how many different possibilities? Okay, I never counted. But just for argument's sake, let's say upwards of twenty, give or take. Believe me, I'm not saying the other nineteen have anything to be ashamed of. But when it comes to Chinks, I say you can't go wrong near the corner of Forty-eighth and Third!

Listen, don't ask me to mention the name. Because one thing they don't need is the publicity. I mean, you talk about your take-out lines, here's where they really invented it. On the other hand, don't kid yourself, you serve an egg roll where the people really know what they're getting, you'll do business, believe me. You take the clientele at Forty-eighth and Third, I guarantee you there are enough of them without any plug from yours truly!

So to make a long story short, I'm fifth in line to get to

the cash register. In other words, I have got my egg roll and it is time to settle up. Sixty-five cents, right? Meaning, maybe I've got it in change. This is when I put my hand in my pocket and it is the pocket Paki is in. Except I'll be honest with you. At this stage of the game, I didn't get it home yet and see what's stamped on the blade yet. So at this stage of the game, let's just say it's just this knife, okay?

The next thing I know, there's this customer ahead of me. To my way of thinking, she is the type of individual a person would notice. In my opinion, a person would. Here's why. Number one, the hair. The reason is, it's hair colored the color of the candy called Turkish Delight. But this is just number one. Long hair the same as the candy. Number two, I could be wrong, but in my opinion this individual is not wearing any underpants.

This is something I always check for.

I walk back in back of them and check for it.

Ninety-nine times out of a hundred, you can tell. So long as it's summer and you're right behind, you can! Believe me, I am not saying anybody can. Far be it from me to talk for somebody else! I am just making reference to my own personal experience. No offense if it's off-color, but the fact is it's a question of the crack. Granted, they all have different types of ones. Take it or leave it, but there are no two cracks which are exactly the same. On the other hand, when they are not wearing their underpants, they are all the same in a certain way!

Okay, you say, "What way?" Whereas I say, "What if I

asked you how you write your bestsellers?" You see what I'm saying? In the final analysis, let's just call it the tricks of the trade or a so-called professional secret or whatever. You have to have yours and I have to have mine. Enough said?

Okay, so here is the mental picture.

To begin with, I go out the door back in back of her.

By the corner of Forty-ninth, I've got mine all chewed and swallowed. Whereas she is just nibbling hers. So she turns toward Second. Nibble, nibble, nibble. She is walking slow. Nibble, nibble, nibble. You know what? A person which is pigeon-toed, it's really funny to see them when they walk slow. Nibble, nibble, nibble. But don't ask me why. It just is.

The other thing is her shoes.

Like they're white and soft.

Hey, I can hear them, white and soft. Like this. Woof, woof, woof. Only slower. Woof. Woof. Woof. More like this and very soft.

Number three, listen to this.

It is her elbows. You know how some people hold them out like this? So the thing of it is, she is one of those people! Out like this. You see what I am saying? In other words, her crack, right? But also her elbows out like this. So this is where the knobs come in. Most cases, the knobs are definitely hidden, okay? Except here's a time they're not. Most cases, they go in where the waist is, only hers are showing, seeing as how the elbows are sticking out!

I'm speaking strictly for myself. But you know what I

say? I say this is interesting. I say you are seeing something you know you are not supposed to! I say you are seeing something which they are always trying to keep hidden! On the other hand, let's say you are in the right place at the right time. You see what I am saying? For example, you take the time they came out dancing. Enough said?

Meanwhile, nibble, nibble, nibble, woof, woof, woof. And then she stops. What she does is she stops. But what's the reason? The answer is a window. Pay attention. This is what she's doing—she is looking in a window!

So I don't know. I mean, it's just a store. If you want the facts, let's face it, I don't remember. The point is, she's nibbling. Here's something else. Even standing still, she is still pigeon-toed!

Myself, I wipe my lips and wipe my fingers.

This is another important thing about the place. Okay, it's sixty-five cents, but consider the extras. Which are a little bag of mustard and a little bag of duck sauce, not to mention a napkin and the wax paper they give you to hold the egg roll with.

Hey, you guessed it.

It's because of the extras that it comes to me how to get up close to her.

This is the mental picture. There is a garbage can in front of the store. Whereas she is standing in front of the store. So this is what I say to myself. If I go throw something in the garbage can, I will be standing right next to where she is.

It is easy. I just go throw the things right in there. I don't say this. I don't say, "Pardon me." I just lift the lid and throw them in. Then I put it down and go like this. You know, like brushing the tips of your fingers.

This is smart. It says, "He is all right." It says, "He is a tidy person and clean and you don't have to run away."

But here is the best thing. I mean, here is how the whole thing of it comes to me—meaning, the word and my trademark and everything.

I brush off my fingers, right? So now what? In other words, I have to do something or how can I stand there? Whereas if I look in the window, then this is the tip-off. So I say to myself I have to do something. Because the thing of it is, you have to look like a person which is strictly all business. You see what I'm saying? I mean, in this pocket, there's Paki. But what about in the other one? So this is when I put my hand in and, lo and behold, what's in it?

Hey, I know I don't have to tell you. *Resuscitate.* It's the word for today from the Word-a-Day calendar!

Bingo, the whole idea just comes to me!

So do you get the mental picture? I look at the page and see the word. But meanwhile it says, "He is an individual who is taking care of business. He is an individual with things on his mind. He is an individual with places to go." You see how doing this says these things?

The next thing is, I put it back. But it goes back in the same pocket as Paki.

Nibble, nibble, nibble. That's her. I mean, she knows it's all right. Aren't I a person with business on their mind?

"Resuscitate." That's me, I just say it. "Resuscitate." Which is when she looks. Like, you know, he said what? Which is when they look and their eyes are wide open.

YOU TAKE SOMEBODY WHO didn't know about the word. He says, "Hello." What happens? He says, "Do you know what time it is, please?" What happens? He says, "Excuse me, is this way east or west?" What happens?

Forget it!

I mean, this is the whole thing about the word.

They look!

They open wide and look.

Bingo, Paki goes in the one on the left.

Enough said?

Okay, so where was I? Time out to look and check.

Hey, how about Forty-ninth, the downtown side between Second and Third?

I'm sorry. That was just another icebreaker. It's the jitters. It's the nerves. I was just kidding, no offense intended. Big deep breaths, okay? I know how long a minute is. I will just stop and take some deep ones. Time out, okay?

All right. All right. Time in again! Time in again!

So the thing of it is, it's no big deal aside from what I said. Except you sometimes hear a click. But you can't really see anything because the goo gets in the way. The fat one, I saw something there, all right. But that one was the one time I did, and I'll be honest with you—I say, "Thank God." The other times, it's nothing much. At least it is not what you'd expect. It's just some goo and stuff and Paki's handle. I mean, the thing is, the handle's in the way. Whereas so far as what you hear goes, that's a different question altogether. Sometimes there is this click, okay?— and other times there isn't.

My own theory is it could be this or it could be that. The click, I mean. Okay, it's maybe she's got on contacts, which is one idea. But I'm not one hundred percent convinced. For instance, it could be you maybe hear a pop and it comes out sounding like a click. So you say to me, "A pop? What pops?" And I say to you it's maybe the eyeball or the brain. But let's face it, this is one for the experts. Myself, I never made a study of the subject. But just for argument's sake, like there could be this skin or shell or something. You see what I mean? Like with a grape maybe. I mean, there's maybe this thing which goes around like a rind on the brain. So Paki pops it open and you get like a little noise. A click. Except you only hear it sometimes. On the other hand, this could be because you don't always stop to think to yourself it is time for you to listen close.

Hey, you tell me. To my way of thinking, this subject is a mystery. Look at it this way—first you think this, then you think that, whereas the next thing you know you are thinking something else. For example, I'm sitting here thinking, and a whole new theory just comes to me. Which is that all of the time maybe all it is is bone! You see what I am saying? I mean, a simple thing like this! Except it's a question of you can't see Peter for Paul!

Listen, forget it. What we are talking about is your average midtown Gotham lunch hour. So it's a madhouse, right? No kidding, you're lucky if you can hear yourself think!

So that's it and that's it—except for getting Paki out and back shut down and put away before she falls and the people in the public come to take a look. But don't kid yourself. You don't really have to hurry really. It's dead. I mean, she is. But if she's set right when you jab her, she can stand and stand. You'd be surprised. I'm not talking minutes, of course. I just mean it is not like okay you do it and here she comes flopping down on you before you have a chance to catch your breath. In other words, she's going to stay on her feet for maybe upwards of five, ten, fifteen seconds, give or take. But it all depends on how she's set, all things being equal. I don't know. Maybe one with big you-know-whats, maybe one of those would tip over faster. But up to now I don't see where the question of the you-know-whats has come into it. Like I said, there's nothing out of the ordinary so far—so long as you leave that fat one out of it. I mean, hey, the way it just kept coming out and out. Like a lump sort of, only with these bubbles behind it pushing it out.

So that's the whole deal right there. The rest is turn around and pick a place and keep going.

I picked Forty-ninth and First. I mean, the first time I did it, this is the place I picked. You know, I picked Peartree's. It wasn't so far away and I still had some of my lunchbreak left, so I said to myself, "Let's make it Peartrees." Except, to tell you the truth, I didn't put a lot of thought into it!

SO THERE YOU GO INSOFAR AS THE TIME when yours truly comes that close to asking for one once. I mean, I almost said, "Gary, make mine a pink peppered vodka just like Mr. C." But long story short, I didn't. What I had was my usual instead, which is a Coke with a twist of lemon. Whereas the thing is, I think a cream soda would have been just what the doctor ordered. Only they don't handle those kind of beverages there. Or if they do, Gary is keeping the truth to himself. I mean, my stomach was in a state from when I swallowed the egg roll so fast. Let's face it, it was acting up. Live and learn, right.

Like you take what they say when they come in and ask you the three questions. Or when they come in and say, "Drink it." Listen, don't kid yourself! Yours truly was there! I promise you, I know what I am talking about!

So tell me the truth, when I thought of the thing of the word, I really thought of something, didn't I? But forget it. Meaning, believe me, I am definitely not asking for any credit for it. Granted, to begin with, it was more or less an accident. Only who knows? Maybe it wasn't. I mean, look at it this way. Every morning yours truly tiptoes in and tears off the page for the day, which is so that this way I can test you-know-who on it when there comes time for it when it's at night. So the day in question is just like any other day, right? So I tiptoe in. I get the page. I blow him a kiss because this way he can keep on getting some more of his forty winks without the kiss waking him up. Then I put the page in my pocket and tiptoe out. Okay, so here is the mental picture. The page is in my pocket and a certain somebody is on their way to Midtown. Only the thing is, this is the day when yours truly spots Paki!

I don't know if I told you, it's a walk-up, five flights not counting the first. But I'll be honest with you, the boy is looking forward to better things. In other words, this was the start of something big! On the other hand, don't think I made the media right off the bat. I mean, with *resuscitate*. Like I said, in this day and age you are crazy if you expect to. Listen, there are no shortcuts. There are no substitutes! You are either ready to work your way up or forget it!

I figure it this way. There is only so much room to go around, whereas meanwhile there is all of this stuff which is always going on. I don't care who you are, every individual has to work hard and wait their turn!

Come on, I paid my dues! Which even the media could see by the time of *scintilla*. You take *scintilla,* this is the one when yours truly starts breaking into print and also all over the channels. Let's just say for openers the following. The *Post*! Channel 5! Channel 9! Nothing national yet, okay.

But in my personal opinion the *Post* is top coverage so far as your local media goes. Whereas I would be the first one to admit it, the *Times* is your ultra situation. Let's face it, did any of the famous celebrities make it into the *Times* overnight? Check it out! Did Berkowitz? Did Bundy? Did Speck? Hey, don't make me laugh.

Naturally, all this is a long way from Channel 13 and *Newsline*, Catherine Campion reporting. But I don't have to tell you, they came around. They could see who meant business. So when they see it, they give me the nod over there also. Whereas Sue Cott and Channel 2, forget it! Meaning, pretty as T.C. says Sue is, let's put it this way— that deal is nothing on the order of your ultra! In other words, you don't exactly have to knock yourself out before Channel 2 can see where it makes sense to give you a tumble. They're in the business. They know what side their bread is buttered on! Hey, in this day and age, who doesn't?

LISTEN, I'M NO PHILOSOPHER, far from it. But I say it's all the same deal in this day and age. With your two major exceptions. Which are money, number one, and safety from bodily harm, second! These two are where you got some individuals which are trying to get a corner on the market. Put it this way—certain persons have too many pegs for their own good. Okay, this is just one man's opinion. But let's not forget I know what I'm talking about!

Notice, yours truly is not mentioning any names. On the other hand, I am not saying present company didn't make mention of some of the right ones when he wrote a certain famous story about a certain famous dining establishment on Fifty-fifth Street west of Madison Avenue! Hey, I for one take my hat off to a certain famous celebrity, seeing as how he wasn't afraid to call a spade a spade!

Whereas you take me. I'm no genius. Neither could you say I've got all the answers. But let's face it, there is a certain party in my household, right? So considering this certain party, you know what I say? I say this party is going to get his share of the pegs, end of discussion, period!

Okay. Enough said. That's as far as I go with philosophy. I'm just saying it is high time I give myself a little credit. I mean, stop and ask yourself, who figured all of this out? You think I just sat around here waiting for T.C. to think it up for me? Hey, the facts are the facts! She's got her *Charlie's Angels*. Which is not to mention some other things I could go ahead and maybe make reference to if I was the type of an individual who talks off-color!

But here's the thing.

The boy.

Just don't make me have to remind you!

On the other hand, let's not forget some other things, which is the question of Janet Rose and my dad.

Okay, they're where?

You see what I am saying?

Now stop to think for a minute. The book comes out. It says so forth and so on. It says this is the authorized story of so-and-so, the famous you-know-what, the individual who did it forty-seven times, which is the new Gotham record! Add to this the thing of the eyeball, always the left one. Plus the whole deal is what? The answer is, the whole deal is exclusive! And then you ask yourself this—so who's got the exclusive? In other words, is it just some wordsmith who went to college or is it the top man in the biz!

You see what I am getting at?

I mean, what then? So they see it and then what?

I guarantee you, wherever they are, those two of them are going to be on the next boat! With bells on!

Hey, you think yours truly doesn't know what he is talking about? Listen, don't make me die laughing.

SO WHEN IT COMES TO A TITLE, what do you think? Or am I going too fast for you at this stage of the game? I don't know—in my personal opinion, it pays off to think ahead.

Myself, I'm thinking in terms of something short and snappy. Like maybe how about *Fascination*?

Hey, don't get huffy. So far as the title goes, I would be the first one to tell you this is your end of the business. I promise you, I have got enough headaches already. Believe me, I am not sticking my nose in where it is definitely not wanted.

Did it look like I was trying to butt in on you into your

department? I wouldn't blame you if you had your feelings hurt! Don't kid yourself, when it comes to between the two of us, yours truly knows which one the wordsmith is! But I am not exactly a moron, okay? I mean, it might surprise you if I told you all of the ways I have improved myself. Number one, there's vocabulary, as I don't think I have to say. What I also don't have to tell you is this. Yours truly knows he is definitely not perfect. To begin with, I'll be honest with you, I never got all of the way through school. Okay, I had to give it up for professional reasons, but this is another story. The facts are the facts, and I for one am not trying to sweep them under the carpet. Meaning, number one, there is an assortment of deficiencies in my educational background. But in certain departments I have gone as far as you can go in self-improvement! Vocabulary I already made mention of. The bank and radio—here again you don't need reminding. Channel 13 yours truly made reference of when the opportunity came up. Also, my reading material is of the highest caliber. So do yourself a favor and don't count me out. I guarantee you, whatever the situation, two heads are better than one!

In Cold Blood. That's good. I was all for it. But this one you used already. *Executioner's Song*. Okay, that one's definitely out. I mean, ask yourself, does it get the message across? On the other hand, it's got some class. But let's face it, by now it's behind the times. *Son of Sam*, on the other hand, here's your real grabber. Okay, I am just a layman, but this is my honest opinion. So maybe you know the individual who wrote it, this Lawrence D. Klausner by name. Hey, no offense. I am just sitting here thinking in which direction I can help you out. So here is my advice. Maybe you and Larry should break bread together and just kick it around. I mean, you never know. The way I see it, it does not hurt for you to spend a few dollars to get the benefit of a person's thinking, famous celebrity or otherwise!

Authorized.

It's like Mutual, only different. I mean, authorized is solid, it makes you feel good, but not sleepy and good in how it is I mean it when I sit here and make reference with you to Ben Bernie.

To make a long story short, this is where I got it from. Which is off the cover of Larry's book. Like this. *Son of Sam*, Based On The Authorized and so forth and so on.

In my analysis, it's this particular word which makes it a hot item.

Authorized.

Listen. Authorized.

Hey, like camisole, right? I mean, talk about your powerful vocabulary, those fellows had it!

You know. "Do you see the thing with the laces? It is called a camisole. Now answer the three questions or we are going to take you and put you in it."

Or paraldehyde. There is another one which really has some meat and beef to it.

Okay, forget it. I was just throwing authorized out there to you to give you something to play around with.

Like, *Fascination*, right?

By the way, you know this Larry K. or what? True or false, you and Larry break bread together at the C.B. together? No offense to anybody, but I would like to see this Berkowitz match his Larry against my Truman. Let's face it, this is like ringtoss on the same boardwalk as Fascination! Or let's just say a certain junior party in my household racing some rich colored on a tenner!

Sure, she beat him. But you tell me. It's fair—only just three gears against ten of them?

Or what about Davie against the whole Atlantic Ocean!

Come on, let's not kid ourselves. I mean, is this ridick or is this ridick?

All right, one thing I don't have to tell you is poker is just poker. In other words, so you play it with balls and these lights light up. Meanwhile, the thing of it is, what's the nature of your color caller? Let's not forget, it is your color caller who is your individual which gets them in off of the boardwalk!

Listen, here's the thing with calling color. It's personality, end of discussion, period. In other words, it's personality and that's it. You think Bill Lido didn't know a good thing when he saw it? Believe me, Bill was a professional!

"This is the world's largest network, the Mutual Broadcasting System."

That was Bill Lido. The man was the best and don't let them tell you any different!

You know what I think? Let's just say they had let me back on the airwaves. Okay, they didn't, but if they did. You see what I'm saying? This is just one man's opinion, but let's not forget who's talking.

Or you take Buddy Brown. I mean, what if she put up a picture of yours truly next to the one of him so you really could get a good look at the both of them together!

I don't know. It makes me feel fast inside to get involved with you in a discussion of this type.

I think I better slow down. I'll be honest with you, I think I have been going too fast.

Ben Bernie. Hey, Ben Bernie. Talk about the individual who could slow you down!

Remember? Remember Ben Bernie and his band? Hey, who in his right mind could ever forget the Old Maestro? God love him, Ben Bernie could really slow you down.

The way he used to do his sign-off, it was like this voice which is putting you to sleep and pulling the covers up to your chin. *A bit of a this and a bit of a that,* he used to say. *A bit of a this and a bit of a that* and so forth and so on. Hey, you remember? All of these good-byes and these good-nights he would say to you in all these different foreign languages?

Ben Bernie.

Ben Bernie was the greatest thing there ever was.

You heard him, and you could really believe it. I mean, like there was this person right inside of the radio. Even his name, for crying out loud. It made you feel like it was back before she went to business and used to let you watch her sewing. I'll be honest with you, that's how Ben Bernie made me feel. Ben Bernie made me feel like nothing I could ever tell you. But you know what I mean.

Listen, I am going to sit and tell you this one thing as far as Ben Bernie, fair enough?

He was the best friend a certain somebody ever had!

Au revoir, auf wiedersehen, good-night and pleasant dreams.

Okay, so I don't remember it exactly how he said it. But don't worry, this is definitely not a permanent situation. Believe me, it is just a question of waiting until it is ready. A thing like this you can't hurry. In other words, when it is ready for it to let you remember it, then this is when you will, end of discussion, period!

Hey, Ben Bernie, Ben Bernie. Am I right or am I right? The Old Maestro. Boy, do I miss him!

LISTEN, WHAT DOESN'T COME BACK when it gets good and ready? Take Janet R. or my dad, for example. Believe me, you are sitting there wasting your breath if you say anything to the contrary.

Put it this way. You get the book all typed up and give it to Random House. So then it comes out and it's this unbelievable bestseller. The next thing which happens is they see you on Johnny's looking at you talk to Johnny about it. So Johnny asks you all of these questions about what they did to me after they caught me, and meanwhile the people in the public in the television audience are listening. In other words, Johnny wants to know the name of the place where they're keeping me. This is when you tell him. But guess who else is listening! Those two of them, they could be anywhere, as it goes without saying, but doesn't everybody everywhere sit and listen to Johnny?

Okay, it's just the mental picture I have. But this does not mean you can't depend on it. Hey, can you just see their faces when they see me! First, we kiss and hug. Then when everybody catches their breath, I will give them a little time-out for them to make their excuses. They'll go, "We did not know where to find you, but now this is ancient history." Then there will be some more kissing and more hugging. The only hard part is going to be which one I kiss and hug the most. So what is your thinking on this, my dad or Janet R.? I don't know. I am going to have to think about it some more. The thing is to keep thinking it through enough.

"Do you read me, Red Dog? This is Blue Dog calling, come in!"

Here's something. I just thought of this. Yours truly is more or less the same as Ben Bernie so far as the boy and his pocket goes. Okay, so let's face it, Ben Bernie was the one and only! But in a manner of speaking, isn't yours truly? Plus the other thing is when I do you-know-what with Paki. I mean, I try to handle it the way the Old Maestro would—slow and mellow and more or less like easy come, easy go, easy on, easy off.

This is Ben Bernie saying good-night.

Talk about the greatest thing which ever was!

Effectuate.

Disdain.

Resuscitate.

Scintilla.

It's like the calendar is the script and like yours truly is signing them off the way Ben Bernie did—just so slow and so mellow and so dreamy and nice.

Au revoir, auf wiedersehen, a bit of a this and a bit of a that and good-night.

You watch. I'm telling you it's going to come back to me! Let's face it, the whole deal is out there where everything else is. It's like dust, if you know what I mean. It's like it's only a question of when it gets ready to blow over to where you happen to be when it gets ready to do it.

Like Janet Rose the night she shows up at Fascination with yours truly calling color. You know what? She just stood there. I mean, you had these loops the different color callers worked, so I am working mine. Let's say it's nine to ten, eight to nine, somewhere in this neighborhood. So she stands there through my whole loop. I'm not saying she played. You see what I'm saying? I'm saying she just stands there watching you-know-who. You think I'm going overboard, but God is my judge, she was. In other words, she was only thirteen, but you don't know the half of it!

Correction: Not through my whole loop exactly. To begin with, I was into it for a while before I see her. So maybe she wasn't there until I did. And the other thing is this. She goes off for a minute and comes back with a cone. So let's say it wasn't the whole loop. But it was more or less the same difference!

Did I tell you your frozen custard was just starting to make it with the people in the public that summer? It was like your cha-cha-cha. This was when they were both of them getting hot with the people in the public. At least with the ones of them on the Long Beach boardwalk they were—a certain type of dance and new dessert favorite.

Hey, but what did a frozen custard cost in that day and age? A nickel? Tops, a dime? You see what I mean?

SHE FRENCHES ME THE NIGHT I'm telling you about. She Frenches me just the way I see her French her frozen custard—which is off-color, but like it or lump it!

You think her mouth was still cold from it? I don't remember. Maybe it was. I don't know. But this is not why I will never forget it any of the times she did it, first time definitely included!

I heard somewhere where some of your opposite gender put ice in their mouth before they do it. But let's face it, with Janet R. you wouldn't need it. I'm telling you, she was in a class by herself. Whereas I am not saying ice is not interesting in and of itself. Except yours truly can't see it in this particular connection.

To my way of thinking, ice makes whatever it is worse. Like the boys in your bestseller who killed the family. Just stop to think about it. They did it indoors. But let's say they didn't. I mean, just for argument's sake, let's say they took them outside and did it on the ice. You see the difference?

It's different on ice. Don't ask me why, but it is!

In my analysis, your movie people and your television people are all wet in connection with this particular department. They don't know what the real thing is—how it goes fast and slow at the same time and looks floppy if you look at it right. But let's face it, your average individual is a total layman in this department. According to my theory, your average individual thinks the movie thing or the television thing is what they are going to see when the wave comes. Am I right or am I right? Whereas the mental picture they are waiting for is all wet from the word go. This is why the real thing looks so funny-looking to them! You see what I am saying? The laymen in the public don't know how to see it because they never saw it before!

This is the thing with Janet R. In other words, when we go get on the beach. What I'm saying is, it was funny-feeling because it was real! Just take the way she took her shoes off and how she moves her legs and arms when she's doing it. I mean, this wasn't anything anybody ever saw before!

Here's another thing. Which is how her head goes when

she gets going with the Frenching. It's like your you-know-what is the microphone and she is trying to get in the right position to talk into it!

It is a question of things being where they are supposed to be—this I don't have to tell you. If something is a pica off in any department, forget it!

Listen, only Janet R. could fill you in on this. Myself, I am not the expert. But for what it's worth, it's how you breathe. Let's face it, everything is. The whole thing is this. It's getting the deep breaths and holding them in!

I'll be honest with you. If anybody could breathe better than Bobby R. could, they would have to name Janet Rose the one individual which could do it!

Okay, this was the thing she could do better than any-body, and don't let anyone tell you different. A girl who could do what Janet R. could is a girl in a class by herself!

And let's not forget something else. She says she's four-teen, but she isn't. Whereas you and I know she is thirteen the all-important summer I am talking about. God is my judge, thirteen!

But what's the diff one way or the other? I mean, sup-pose she was the same age T.C. turned last birthday. You think age is your factor here? Believe me, when it comes to Frenching you, age is definitely out of the picture. Whereas face it, you haven't even heard about the mirror yet!

OKAY, TIME OUT. I MADE A MISTAKE to wait so long to get to this particular subject. It's this thing of ages.

So the question is, how should you handle it when you get down to typing it up? Time flies, take it or leave it. This is why I say there is no time like the present!

Let's not kid ourselves. The minute I mention it, I start getting hot under the collar from it. But at this stage of the game, do I have to pull any punches? Let's put it this way, I am really beginning to feel good with you. I'm here to tell you, I don't know how you did it, but God is my witness, you did. Do you see what I am saying? Because at this particular stage of the game, I am beginning to feel I can let my hair down with you. Let's be honest with each other. I had my doubts. But that's all water under the bridge.

So it's time to talk turkey, okay?

What I am doing isn't nice, and yours truly knows it. But so far as present company is concerned, I know I don't have to explain myself. End of discussion, period.

On the other hand, so long as we understand each other, I want you to know I do not shy away from criticism. In other words, I've got a lot to learn, and I would be the first one to admit it! But there is one particular item which is definitely out of bounds with me. And for your information, I don't want to hear one more word about it!

As regards this particular item, let's not kid ourselves. You have already heard the media's personal opinion. Fair enough. But before you say one word on the subject, I think it is only simple decency for you to give yours truly a chance to tell his side of the story.

To begin with, I am acting within very strict guidelines. I have nothing against anyone personally. So far as myself is concerned, business is business and everything else is like, you know, like prologue.

Okay. So far, so good.

Now, to my way of thinking, forty-seven makes sense as regards the cutoff on the total. Whereas in the same vein of thinking, it also makes sense to establish a lower limit with regard to the age of any particular individual.

This I did. Right off the bat, I said to myself, "Let's establish a lower limit with regard to the age of this or that particular individual, all things being equal."

I promise you, this was my policy from the word go.

Do you follow me so far?

Okay, so well and good.

Now, I don't have to tell you what I am working with is guesswork. This is just for openers. Number two, various different other factors enter in.

Fine, so live and learn. So a handful of times because of this, that, and the other thing, I maybe guessed a little wrong with regard to the age factor. In other words, the media comes out with the actual statistics, yours truly sees where sometimes the individual in question was still in the so-called teens. So like I said, live and learn.

Naturally, it goes without saying, yours truly is sitting here taking the media's word at face value.

Enough said.

So now to get down to cases. You read the papers. You watch the channels. What they are saying is no secret. But I say don't jump to conclusions which are unsubstantiated until you give me an honest appraisal.

Do you want my personal analysis?

This is what Norman didn't do. I could have talked myself blue in the face, but the man's mind was made up on the subject, end of discussion, period. All right, it is a free country. To my way of thinking, the man was entitled to an explanation, whereas no one can say it was not forthcoming. Meanwhile, if he holds it against me, then he holds it against me. So if this is the price you have to pay for being aboveboard, I for one am only too happy to pay it!

I just want you to know my thinking is clear as regards this particular item. Number one, it's raining. Number two, the word is *cellulose*. Number three, was she really fifteen or is this just what the media is saying? My recommendation is this—maybe the media has its reasons for lying. Because it wouldn't be the first time, would it?

But one way or the other, let's go back to the beginning. Like I said, there are your various different factors. The particular word for the day, to begin with. What it's doing in there I couldn't begin to tell you. To my mind, it doesn't belong in the boy's calendar in the first place!

Second, it's a Friday. So why is a Friday special? Number one, it is the day before I get two days all alone with you-know-who. Number two, it's the deadline for handling the

time charts and for posting the paychecks for the Friday following. Number three, it's the traffic. Meaning, your smart
money is beating it out of town for the weekend.

And did I make mention of the rain yet? Hey, forget it!

Okay, so all of this adds up to your so-called pressure.

Not that yours truly can't handle pressure.

But think of it this way. One of your bestsellers gets
delivered to the printer. It is a cinch it is another classic.
Still and all, in your heart of hearts, there are these pres-
sures, etc., etc. Am I right or am I right?

So here are certain factors to begin with. Granted, nothing major—but you still cannot just go ahead and sweep
them under the carpet.

Okay, so next we come to the biggest one. And in this
connection, I'm sorry but there is no getting around it. In
other words, we are talking about a subject which is definitely off-color. Meanwhile, I promise you, I will try to
give it the once-over-lightly.

Wednesday night is the night per usual. Meaning, this is
the routine night for you-know-what in my particular
household. Whereas you take the week in question, it
turns out Thursday I have to make an exception. The
result is that T.C. and yours truly make amends, granted,
which is the point of the thing in the first place. But the
other thing is my tongue. Do you see what I am saying?

Correction: Not the tongue, but the thing which is
down in there underneath it. In other words, the thing

which goes ahead and keeps it attached to the bottom.

So Wednesday I do her per usual. This means front and back to the best of my ability. But then, lo and behold, come Thursday, T.C. has one of her outbursts. So the upshot is, the thing which is underneath does not have enough time for itself for it to get back to normal.

Okay, here is the mental picture.

These teeth down here, these little ones down in front, no way you can do what I have to do and not get the thing under there all torn up from getting rubbed over the little teeth at the bottom! Let's face it, it takes a week for it to get back to normal. I guarantee you, one week minimum!

So now listen to this and see what you think. It's Thursday night. The TV is going right here in the kitchen, Channel 13 doing the honors. Meanwhile, I and mine are putting supper on the table. The picture is this. The boy is washing the forks. T.C. is getting the milk out. Whereas yours truly is shutting off the oven because the timer says the Swansons are ready. The way I see it, everything is copacetic. This is a happy family getting ready to eat their supper. But the next thing you know, T.C. is going, "Lord, Lord, I am sick to death of you and of everything in this kitchen!"

I go, "Sweetheart, little pitchers have big ears. We will have a discussion of this subject later."

She goes, "Let's not and say we did!"

I go, "Chicken dinners, everybody! Everybody get a nice fresh napkin and sit down at your place at the table!"

She goes, "We ain't sitting nowhere! Him and me are clearing out right this goddamn minute!"

TO MAKE A LONG STORY SHORT, T.C. has these outbursts. Granted, they are nothing for anybody to get in an uproar about. To my way of thinking, it is just a question of holding your breath until the whole affair blows over.

Meanwhile, the Swansons are getting cold, you-know-who is missing *Newsline*, and T.C. is getting worse by the minute. So as it goes without saying, when all is said and done, there is only one way you can get back into the woman's good graces. So true or false, or true or false?

Just between you, me, and the lamppost, I say the thing of it with T.C. is too much nervous tension. For what it's worth, this is my personal analysis. Number one, the job she has to go to and also the fact that the subway scares her. Number two, whatever she says to her way of thinking, I say T.C. still misses Salem. Number three, the State of the Union and the thing it has been doing to yours truly's budget. Number four, the question of the boy's educational experiences—because so far as this question goes, let's face it, T.C. and me are on two different levels.

So let's not kid ourselves. Meaning, yours truly says to himself forget the condition my tongue is in. In other words, marriage is a give-and-take situation. So first I give her the front and then I give her the back, but not until she says, "Hold the phone." Which is what T.C. says when it is time for her to roll over and for her to get her finger down there.

Enough said?

But like I said, the upshot is, come Friday morning, when a certain person starts feeling what his tongue feels like, he could scream bloody murder. You see what I am saying? Marriage is marriage, but the thing under there under the tongue there was not ready for another situation!

I'll be honest with you, the thing of it is this with T.C. As regards either side, you have to reach with your tongue all of the way in there. In words of one syllable, you either get it all of the way in there or forget it, end of discussion, period. The thing you have to do is keep doing it until T.C. says it. Like this. "Hold the phone." So then she rolls over for you to do the back while she goes at it with her finger.

Hey, believe me, yours truly is definitely not complaining. It goes without saying, the mother of the boy deserves every consideration first, last, and always! But meanwhile, when the teeth which your tongue gets rubbed on are thrown into the bargain, a week is what it needs under there between your various episodes of this description!

So getting back to the Friday in question, the toothpaste is where it begins with. Add to this, I make my tea and forget to leave out the lemon. Third, I get to the branch and it hurts too much for yours truly to even say good-morning.

Now, do I have to go back and go over all of these factors for you all over again or was a word to the wise sufficient? Forget it, I already talked myself blue in the face with that, you know, that Norman!

So where are we? Friday of the week in question. In this pocket I've got Paki and *cellulose*—whereas in the other, there is the seven-watter per usual. Meanwhile, my co-workers have a right to expect an iota of courtesy. But can yours truly open his mouth to give it to them? On top of this, there is the rain and the time charts plus this, that, and the other.

The next thing you know, it is the lunchbreak.

So here is the part you are entitled to hear from my side of the story, irregardless of versions to the contrary. I am not saying everyone does not have a right to his or her personal opinion. But let us not forget something.

Yours truly was the only (joke) eye-witness, ha ha.

HEY, HOLD IT, HOLD IT, HOLD IT!

That was way out of line and I know it. God is my judge, I'm really sorry. Honest, I really deserve hail Columbia for that one. But okay, it was just a slip of the tongue. I mean, forget it, I'm just jumpy again, and this is what happens—I get too speeded up and start saying these things which sound like a crazy man. Hey, blame it on Everett. It was Everett which taught me about icebreakers.

You'll see. I'll get to Everett.

I don't know. I think I am getting the jitters again. Okay. Okay. Deep breaths, deep breaths. Time out for yours truly to get calm and collected again.

Ben Bernie. Hey, Ben Bernie.

This is Ben Bernie saying good-night and pleasant dreams.

It's just this thing of having to tell you about the one I did which they are saying was under-age. I mean, stop to think. My tongue, right? Two nights in a row, right? Listen, when I say you have to reach to get T.C. for her to get to have her finish, I am not just robbing Peter to pay Paul, you know!

But okay, okay. Getting back to the one which was *cellulose,* it's raining cats and dogs. So maybe it was the umbrella which made me notice. Meaning, she did not have one. Second, she has these shoes you just step into—clip clop, clip clop, like a horse, you know?

In other words, I am coming out the main entrance and there she is, clip clop, clip clop, cutting across Lex right through all of this Friday craziness, not using the corner and the walk sign in accordance with the lawful regulations. Granted, the traffic is not budging, which it never does in Gotham when there is something by way of a little precip in the picture. Whereas the Friday in question, it is coming down like you-know-how, as I don't have to tell you.

So yours truly crosses right behind her in back of her.

Did you ever see a lassie go this way and that way and this way and that way?

I don't know. This is what she makes me think of, how she is moving her you-know-what this way and that way to get through the vehicles. So I ask you, does a person of what they say her age was have a right to go around and walk like that? Leaving Janet R. herself aside, you tell me, fifteen years old and the gall to go around in the public going this way and that way like that!

In other words, whichever way you turn, there is a different factor. Oh no, clip clop, clip clop. Post the checks, do the time charts—pressure, pressure, pressure! I guarantee you, it's a madhouse! The rain is just to begin with! You want the mental picture? Here is the mental picture. Umbrellas, umbrellas, umbrellas! And meanwhile clip clop, clip clop! Plus my tongue, my tongue!

So first she goes into a shoe repair and yours truly watches through the window.

Hey, you remember what my favorite thing to do is? Hint: Don't forget the Plymouth!

It's just I get so hot under the collar.

So long story short, she takes off her belt and she hands it to a colored behind the counter. Then she stands around and stands around, and then she goes and sits down in one of the special seats they have for when you are getting heels or something. Or (joke) grommets, ha ha.

Maybe you're forgetting this. Did I have anything in my stomach yet? Could I even eat it if I tried? So where was my egg roll this particular Friday! And do I have to tell you I am standing getting soaked while a certain person is sitting down where it is dry?

The thing about her was she had a good hairdo.

She goes to the Pathmark next. Hey, you know the one! At Third and Fifty-second? That one!

I say to myself, "She is in there getting Maybelline." But I can't see her through the glass. Did I tell you she has got this hair which is like there is a fuzzy ball on top? I say to myself, "How come it stays there like this when it is raining cats and dogs like this?" This is interesting. I wish I could have found out how. But bygones is bygones.

Listen, I'll be honest with you, the rain is making everything go fast.

It's just a face when I get a good look at it. Meaning, here she comes back out and it's nothing special, except she looks old enough if she looks a day! Meanwhile just clip clop, clip clop, on up to the corner with you-know-who taking care of his end of it and staying right up back behind her close behind her.

This is when I switch the umbrella over. You know, like from this hand to the other one.

Guess why.

Hey, what a madhouse, what with the horns honking and the splashing splashing and everything stuck and not going anywhere but going fast.

To my way of thinking, there's maybe two dozen people in the public on this side, plus ditto on the other, waiting to cross over. She's this far away from me. I mean, yours truly could reach out his fingers and put them in the ball of fuzz. But forget it! One thing I do not do is something which is crazy. Let's face it, touch it just to touch some fuzz?

I say to myself, "When the walk sign changes."

You know, it is broad daylight but this is Midtown and who notices? Whereas with the rain, they would not notice even if you sent them an engraved invitation! Hey, let us not not kid ourselves. It comes down like this in Gotham, all the people in the public are thinking is, "Don't put my eye out with your umbrellas!"

I put Paki in hers.

I did not even have to turn her around with *cellulose*.

Here's why.

The sign changes. Then there's all these Gothamites crossing over, all this crazy honking and crazy splashing. But you-know-who is standing there not budging!

So neither does yours truly!

I say to myself, "Stay put." I say to myself, "Stay right where you are because a certain person is changing her mind and is going to turn around." Which, bingo, is when guess who does it, turns, and I say, "Cellulose."

Hey, then it's just a question of this—you've got two handles and you have got to hold on to them both!

LISTEN, I WAS JUST AS PERTURBED as everyone else when I read she was the age they said. But live and learn, okay? I mean, at this stage of the game, it's ancient history. Am I right or am I right? Believe me, in my dreams I am still getting the mental picture! You know, clip clop, clip clop. But can yours truly wave a wand? What am I, a magician or just an individual which has a position in Payroll? Granted, a top-ten bank is a top-ten bank, but there are limits!

Cellulose. I mean, forget it! If I had half the brains I was born with, I would have skipped this one for the next one.

But with my luck, it would have been a worse one, right? Take it or leave it, not even Bobby R. could do a thing with *cellulose*—and let's not forget who he was!

Hey, I just thought of something.

True or false, Mason Adams was Pepper Young.

Remember when Pepper used to say, "Aw, heck, Pegs"? Pegs was Pepper's sis.

You know what? It would be nice to be in Pepper Young's family. I mean, let's just think about how nice, how nice.

It would be like Ben Bernie talking all of the time—the Old Maestro saying good-night to you morning, noon, and night to you. Like this—like "Aw, heck, Pegs."

That's nice.

God, how I loved all of those programs! But you take in this day and age, where are they? I mean, it's like with Janet Rose and my dad. So you tell me, does it add up or does it add up?

I don't know. I get so sleepy when I think a thing like this!

SO LONG AS I MADE MENTION of sleepy, you might as well know this is how it was back in the days of Janet R. Meaning sleepy, I mean. Except it was different because it was all of these different opposite ways at once. In other words, you have these people in the public and there they are, far off. Whereas when you look, they're close up! So the question is how it happens—and I say glass is the reason it does.

Look at it this way. Is glass like water or is glass like water? Here is the one difference—water doesn't break!

Hey, skip it. I mean, this is really crazy. God is my judge, I am just sitting here making all of this stuff up.

"Darn it, Pegs, what the Sam Hill is the poor sap saying?"

Question: Who does this remind you of?

Here's something. Think of Pepper Young saying custard. You see what I am saying? Think of Pepper saying that!

She just licked and licked it. Meaning, first the frozen custard and then my you-know-what. The thing of it is, there wasn't any so-called talk. Let's face it, we didn't have to. Not that there was not your usual per usuals—how old you are, what school you go to, where you live, what your parents do for work. But all this is for is for you to keep things going while you get from up on the boardwalk to under it. In other words, keep talking so you can keep doing something else. Which is to get a certain someone down on the beach and get busy with her.

Here's the thing with Janet Rose. She lets you see her thoughts! She doesn't have to say things. But she just shows you with the things she does. I don't know. These are dirty thoughts. But they are not what you would call off-color. Do you see what I am saying? Granted, Janet Rose was dirty. But it's not the kind of dirty you ever thought of.

Forget it. It's too hard for you to understand.

Hey, I am getting a boner just trying to explain. I'm telling you, I am sitting here and really getting one.

The thing of it is, her tongue—touching it and touching it to the top of the cone and saying these things when she does. But the words, they do not have anything to do with it. Which is what makes them even dirtier. Do you follow what I am saying when yours truly says this? Listen. You know the words which someone just says to you to say something. So the thing of it is, these are the words which are the dirtiest ones!

She never says, "Let's go under the boardwalk and I will put it in my mouth." She knows that dirty talk isn't talk like that! Don't kid yourself, it is all the difference, what kind of talk is dirty or not. Hey, skip it. It goes without saying, you either know what I am saying or you don't!

This is what happens next. The cone is all gone.

Now watch this.

She touches her lips with the little napkin and then she touches them with it again.

So here is when guess who asks guess who the all-important question.

"You want for me to put it in the basket for you there over there?"

You see how this is really the thing of it?

Meaning, there are the stairs. Whereas there is the garbage can just before you get to them. So you see how this makes it even dirtier? In other words, it is the reason you said it, but you really didn't say so!

It's like this. It's like saying to someone you'll only be a minute and then really being it!

It's dark once we get down the stairs. But what's the big deal about seeing a face? I'll be honest with you. As faces go, they're all fakes. Hey, can anybody help them not to be? Nobody can! Name anybody—they can't!

Here is what I remember next.

She says she is fourteen and yours truly says he is sixteen so as to make a big enough difference. I don't know. Is this when I say my brother is a terrific dancer and dances at one of the hotels? Let's not kid ourselves, who can do it from soup to nuts? It gets hard to do it when yours truly starts getting one of his big boners.

This is when she takes her shoes off. This is when I see her do it. Take it or leave it, but it is not like a thing which I ever saw before or ever once saw since.

Here's something. It's like this is how a girl really does it. It's like this is what she does when she thinks no one is around for them to see her do it. But here is the second thing of it—which is she knows there really is!

Does this make sense or does this make sense?

I mean, it is like seeing something secret. It is like there's the glass, but you do not have to ask when you need to look through it because she really wants you to do it. Hey, you think it is how she lifts her legs up or reaches down to get them off?

Janet Rose's shoes! Janet Rose's shoes and feet!

And let's not forget the other thing, which is Janet Rose's hair.

In words of one syllable, Barbara Luddy!

How's that for a name from the Golden Olden Days! Is that a name from our day and age or is that a name from our day and age? Don't you remember week after week—Barbara Luddy and Olan Soulé?

Mr. and Mrs. First-Nighter. Am I right or am I right?

The thing of it is, this is what you think of—Barbara Luddy's name and Janet Rose's hair. Don't kid yourself. I couldn't give you a better mental picture—the kind of hair I mean. In other words, it's brown and bouncy just like, you know, like Barbara Luddy's name.

You know what? Go look at *Newsline*, Catherine Campion reporting! Whereas for the story on Sylvia Berman's, check out Channel 2 and Sue Cott!

Let's not kid ourselves, these two are the only two types which are even worth mentioning. Whereas faces, forget it from the word go! If anything can throw you off, a face is the first thing which can do it, like it or lump it!

But take feet. Or take shoes.

Shoes is something you can always count on. Not that you also can't do it on feet. So as regards this question and the individual we are talking about, do I have to sit here and tell you? Believe me, this is yours truly telling you the answer is Janet R. is bar none in both departments!

So let's just start with her shoes, just to begin with. It's summer, but the color is what? White like everybody else? Forget it! Meaning, they're not! But the color is not the best part. It is the thin little strap which is!

See if you can see this, this like this little glass window the strap gives you when you look at her feet. In other words, the toes are covered but the beginning of the cracks aren't! It's like these tiny you-know-whats of their privates which you can look through the little window to see them.

To my way of thinking, it is shoes like these which make you think of naked. But do me a favor and don't ask me to tell you why it's this which is the caliber of my thinking. I mean, it could be a question of this or it could be a question of that. Not to mention it could also be the bones and the veins along with the toes and the creases between them!

Hey, am I getting a big boner! I guarantee you, yours truly is really getting a big one.

Okay, okay, big deep breaths for everybody involved!

She puts her arms down. She lifts her legs up. The elbows go in and then the elbows go out.

Did you ever see a lassie go this way and that way and this way and that way?

Sometimes I think of it like this—like the thing on Fourteenth or the one where the man who made the pizzas jumps up. In other words, it's a thing which is real, and this is why it doesn't look it! You take a thing which is real like this, and you know what? You say to yourself somebody is making it up! Because what if somebody isn't?

LET'S FACE IT, CREASES, CRACKS, WHATEVER— just don't make me have to spell it out for you. These are the words and that's that. I mean, guess who just got a boner only from writing them down and not even from saying them out loud.

Here's another thing. She already had you-know-whats. Granted, there's this blue dress with white dots on it. But I could tell even in the dark she already had them under it.

Not that I get to feel them or see them—or do anything else in this particular department. As regards the all-important summer in question, I don't. On the other hand, I don't have to tell you what happens when the summer is over!

Meanwhile, it's still the night I am talking about. In other words, it is the beginning of August.

The thing of it is, she only takes her shoes off. Also, as it goes without saying, there is no feeling anything of hers, end of discussion, period. Do you see what I'm saying? It was okay to give her little kisses. But it wasn't okay to hug her or feel her you-know-whats or touch them where they were.

Here's what she said. She said this was the way to start. She said the thing was to do the thing with her mouth and then she would decide after that. In words of one syllable, the thing with Janet R. was to give you the French thing and then give you another one after that!

Okay, that was uncalled for. That was definitely way off base. Forget I ever said it. I know we do not need this caliber of language, whatever they tell you to the contrary. Believe me, it is a caliber which has no place in a situation like this. I guarantee you, my mind is not in the gutter.

This is one thing I cannot condone, which is a mind which is down there with the rest of them in the gutter! You know as well as I do, I am a man who runs a household, not to mention a former show-business person in my own right. So I naturally know things, as it goes without saying. For example, my experience as regards this department could fill up a shirt cardboard on both sides.

You know what size those cardboards in your shirts are? And I was writing small! In other words, yours truly was not born yesterday. On the other hand, an individual in your circle goes to a French hand laundry, true or false? Whereas your French hand laundries give them back to you on hangers, don't they? So do they or don't they? Listen, I have been around. I know not everybody and his brother has to go to the Chink on the corner!

All right, you caught me at it again. I mean, okay, I wasn't aboveboard one hundred percent. So big deal, T.C. does my shirts here in our place and we don't take them to the Chink's. The thing of it is, that's how it is in banks. Meaning, the dress code which says what you can work in. Whereas your writer, they can write in anything they want to. Take Norman, for instance. You think he has to beg his ball and chain to iron him shirts or not?

Listen, do me a favor and don't make me laugh.

Hey, let's face it, here I am just shooting my mouth off again because I am trying to get rid of this boner. So all right, you can tell, can't you? Listen, if I had half the brains

I was born with, I'd get back to where I was about the part about under the boardwalk. Am I right or am I right? It's just that where the thing of it is, I start going back to it and then start getting myself a new boner all over again!

I mean, come on, a boner in your own kitchen?

Okay, so here we go again—cool as a cuke and all calm and collected again.

These are some of the things Janet Rose told me.

She says her father does something in the dress business. She says he doesn't live with her mother. She says he lives in the city but in a different apartment. She says she's going to go to the Bronx High School of Science. She says she skipped a year so she's going to start with the year after that. She says the Bronx High School of Science is the school for the smartest pupils there are in Gotham.

Listen, check this out before you put it in the book. I mean, about the Bronx High School of Science. In other words, what I'm saying she told me about it, it was how many years ago? Myself, I am in no position to give you the facts on this subject, one way or the other. The thing is, we don't want them shooting us down just because a certain famous celebrity did not do his homework.

I went up there once. It was after I got out of the place the second time. It was the day after that. This is when I saw her walking in the leaves with her you-know-what going this way and that way.

Did you ever see a lassie go this way and that way and this way and that way?

I guess you know the place I am making reference to. Naturally, I cannot make mention of either one of them by name. But this is not for the reason present company is probably thinking. Hey, if I tell you the real one, you swear it won't lower me in your eyes? In other words, don't say it if you don't mean it! Because I honestly think it did it in Norman's.

No offense. Believe me, I am not drawing comparisons.

Okay. The answer is I never asked. Yours truly never asked and no one ever told him!

So this is the answer, take it or leave it.

Hey, what makes you think they put a sign up?

SHE HAS HER SHOES IN HER HAND. She is wearing this dress with white dots. There is this belt which goes around the middle. It's thin and white and tight. It's like the thin little strap which goes across her feet, but not in thinness or in color. But it's still like it.

Her eyes are brown. They are brown. I can't help it. They make me think of the name of Barbara Luddy. Her name is eyes and hair like that.

I was so excited. Just going under the boardwalk did it. Just going under was like saying you were going to do something—because everybody said this was what you went under it for. Meaning, for doing things.

We did not talk about things once we got under there. There was only the one thing which she said. This is what it was. "Lie back." Here is the one thing which I said. "You should see Davie dance." Or maybe it was this instead. "You should see Davie swim." I don't know which one it was.

I don't know. She made me want to say things. I wanted to tell Janet R. everything there was—even about Buddy Brown. It's crazy, but here is the truth. Janet R. was like the sky was hugging me again. It was like the sky was putting down its arms to hug me again but wouldn't snatch me up. Hey, forget it. I mean, I hear myself writing you this, but it just dawns on me, what's words with a thing like this?

It's just too hard for anybody to tell you when, you know, it wasn't your you-know-what in her mouth. It was like the sky before Buddy Brown came along. I didn't have to do anything. She just wanted to get her mouth down on it like it was the sky with its arms. It was like she was all of the things which could not wait to take me and hug me and I was too small to have to hug back.

She says, "Lie back."

Hey, there I go again, not being one hundred percent. I mean, maybe she did not say that. Maybe I just heard it, whereas it didn't have to be said by Janet R. because I and her had ways with each other.

Listen, you think I really thought the voice in the vacuum was not coming from somewhere else? You think I did not know it was? And this goes double for the specks! I mean, how could they really be little animals if every single one of them went the same way at once? Little animals would not do that! I mean, is this ridick or is this ridick?

Here's the thing of it. I look. I listen. Whereas I don't really do either one. Let's face it, who else on Fourteenth heard the things and saw the things yours truly did? But did you-know-who have to try?

I could hear the screams. I could hear the shirts. When the boys threw the paper, who heard it flop?

You think I wanted to?

It made me sleepy. It made me get a little sweaty-feeling and sleepy-feeling and scared.

Even when the police came, I could not stop seeing and hearing and getting even sleepier-feeling.

There was the rack with coats on it. I mean, I saw it. But who else did? I can even smell how the boy with the knife was when he backed up into the rack. I can taste it when he did. I can hear his arm stick out at them and cut them with the knife. I can feel the things which hit him when they did. I can taste the flopping! I can taste it in my ears!

Hey, time out. Time out!

SO I ASK YOU, WHEN IT COMES TO PAKI, where do we stand? Okay, you tell me, are we talking about the big bucks or are we talking about the big bucks?

Look who's asking who! I mean, who wrote the book on this particular subject, present company not excluded?

That's why I was way off base with going to Norman first. True or false, who is the top man—him or you?

So what do you think so far, okay? In other words, just

for argument's sake, suppose I quit right here. Meaning, at twenty-three yours truly calls it a day, end of discussion, period. You think we are already ahead of the game what with twenty-three to the good? Be honest with me. Let's say we called it a day at twenty-three. So if we did, then what's the story? You and the boy get to divvy up what? A million? Five, six? Or am I so far out of the picture I am just talking small potatoes? Because just between you, me, and the lamppost, I would not mind getting a rough idea at this stage of the game. So give me a ballpark. Ten million? Is this too crazy?

On the other hand, make believe I'm already up to *capstone*. So how much for forty-seven instead of for twenty-three? I mean, let's face it, you are the man who wrote the book on this, so talk to me. I am not knocking myself out for nothing, am I?

Hey, do me a favor and don't make me laugh. Don't forget, I was there. I was the one on Fourteenth! I saw the people in the public coming. You couldn't keep them away on a bet! It was standing-room-only! And nobody even got killed even! Whereas yours truly is handing you how many? And I mean signed, sealed, and delivered!

Hint: How old was yours truly last birthday?

She could turn you into water. Her mouth was like being in water. She could make her mouth into water. You were water inside of water. And when you had your finish, you were not even water anymore but were sky anymore. Or even just the color of it.

It was what it was before Buddy Brown or before any-thing in the Buddy Brown department anymore.

She says, "Lie back."

She puts her fingers on my chest and pushes. She says, "Lie back," and pushes me down.

I feel her getting my pants open. I see the cracks in the boards over my head. I know she is getting ready to do something. But I do not know what it is. I can see the cracks and the people in the public walking over them. I can see the shoes walking over the cracks. I can feel her breathing you-know-where. It's breath where I never felt it before.

I can't help it. It's giving me this big boner. It's terrible having what I am telling about, and then you can't ever have it anymore.

Oh, Mr. Capote—please, Janet Rose!

WE SWORE OUR LOVE FOREVER, for always. We kept saying it over and over. This is why yours truly says to present company Mr. and Mrs. First-Nighter.

You do not know what a person feels. With all due respect, who does? No offense, but not even your greatest genius like yourself can get anywhere even near first base!

It's like with Davie—such a swimmer, such a swimmer. But could he get anywhere with that water? Grady couldn't. Namick couldn't. Could even Davie once the water had gone ahead and made up its mind he couldn't?

Go ask Bobby R. to stop vomiting when he had to. Or, hey, how about my dad? I mean, how could he carry his samples around if he didn't have a car to do it? So do me a favor and don't tell me about Davie and the waves! Because the thing of it is, it is God which made the Atlantic Ocean, true or false? So when God gets ready to punish an individual, does even a swimmer stand a chance?

Hey, can a three-speed take a tenner? Come on, couldn't the moron even count?

Listen, I don't have to tell you. So far as any Bronx High School of Science goes, Davie was a dancer and a swimmer, end of discussion, period.

On the other hand, yours truly is such a genius, he was the first one which went in the water!

Okay, so here is the whole thing of it the way yours truly is sitting counting the picas. Let's say it's half for Janet R. and the rest for my moron brother. I mean, did I or did I not owe him a whopper for taking care of Buddy Brown?

So does this make me the moron and not him? Hey, wait a minute, there was a word like this already, wasn't there? Hold the phone a minute. I know! I know! It was the one which went with the fat one where all of the stuff kept bubbling out coming out! Or didn't I tell you about the one which had like the clot? Okay, so maybe it wasn't a clot. So maybe it was like a growth like with like this air in it from like an abscess.

But the word was meanwhile what?

Amentia! Amentia is what the word was!

Hey, how is this for everything coming back!

"Amentia." Then Paki in and Paki out.

She was this messenger. Meaning, she was one of them from this bike service we use for messengers at the bank. Hey, for crying out loud, here's something else! Guess where a certain person was in the process of going to at the particular time I'm talking about! Listen, is this a crazy coincidence or is this a crazy coincidence? Because yours truly was on his way over to Peartree's of all places, when, lo and behold, I spot her and like I see she is walking instead of, you know, riding her bike! So the question is, so why is she doing this? Sure, she wants you to think she is walking it because she has a flat. But I say that's what they all say. Look, let's face it, you should not hire a fat person when you want someone to not get off of a bike!

Not to change the subject, but I will give you three good guesses what I was on my way to Peartree's for.

Go ahead and give up. Because I promise you, you will never guess!

Hint: It was to ask Gary something.

Now do you get it? Because it was to ask guess who about how they get it pink, that type of vodka!

Not that I would ever touch the stuff with a ten-foot pole. It is just that yours truly wanted to know how they did it in case it ever came up. Like suppose you-know-who was to ask me what are those little things flying around? The thing is to have the answer at your fingertips, right? So does this make sense to you or does this make sense to you?

In other words, I'm ready to say the answer is dust! Whereas was anybody ever ready to say it to me? Listen, do me a favor and don't make me laugh! All they ever said to me was they were dancing. But I say dancing in a closet? Come on, who's kidding who, dancing!

Listen, check me out on this, okay? True or false, I have or haven't told you how the word works? I mean, the thing of it is, it makes no sense, which is why it does!

Like this. "Somebody just said to me what?"

But let's face it, did Ben Bernie? Just ask yourself, when the Old Maestro said what he said, didn't you say to yourself, "He said what?" But that's what made it so wonderful! *A bit of a this, a bit of a that,* and so on and so forth. Whereas wasn't it why you listened so hard? Don't kid yourself, when it doesn't make sense is when everybody starts listening!

Like you take your youngsters of today and their songs. So am I right or am I right? On the other hand, it's all a question of keeping up with the times. Like if you take the bestseller about the boys in Kansas and then you take the bestseller about you-know-who in Gotham. So you see how you have to keep up with the times? I mean, look at your own situation, a handful of farmers and they are all in the same family and none of it happened on ice! Whereas look at me and mine, even granted it is only, you know, twenty-three of them so far. You see what I am saying? Don't kid yourself! I don't care who you are, a person has got to keep up with the times!

Not that I envy your youngster of today. Far from it. The streets, for example—whichever way you turn, here comes something, whereas chances are it is bodily harm!

"Red Dog, Red Dog, answer, please!"

A BIT OF A TWEET-TWEET!

This is what Ben Bernie said!

Hey, it just came to me—*a bit of a tweet-tweet*. God is my witness, it came to me just like that!

And then there is something else. It's like *yes sir, yes sir, yes sir.* Or it's like something which is.

Don't worry. It is coming back. It all comes back from wherever it is. You name it, it'll do it—come, come back.

God, how I loved to hear it! It was like how yours truly felt when Janet R. got busy on you with her mouth. Meaning, Ben Bernie swallowed you, every last drop!

She always did it to me once a day minimum. But mostly three or four. She did it all that summer that all-important summer—and even more when the summer was over. It didn't matter where we had to. Janet R. would find a place to. Nights, it was under the boardwalk. Days, we had to look around—parked cars and telephone booths and the ladies' room at the Texaco. It was just a question of her getting you down somewhere or finding a place for her to lean over.

Let's not kid ourselves, this was the summer of summers!

Number one, here comes Janet R. Number two, there goes my dad, and then Davie right behind him.

Pay attention. This is the mental picture.

Yours truly is making good money. And she is still on at McClellan's or wherever. I don't know. So maybe it's a Woolworth's or a McCrory's or a Grant's. What's the diff so long as it's a dimestore? The thing is, she says she is sick and tired of going to business. She says she is fed up right up to here with always having to bust her chops for every kind of colored. She says good riddance to bad rubbish because he never brought in enough to begin with.

These are all quotes I am giving you.

You don't have to bother to check on them for you to be positive. I stand behind them one hundred percent.

Ask Davie.

Hey, no offense! I just thought it was time for another little icebreaker.

Blame Everett. He was always doing these little ice-breakers for people. When they would say "Drink it," and yours truly wouldn't. Or answer the three questions.

Okay, so you can't ask Davie. I mean, I know I don't have to tell you forget it when it comes to Davie.

Hey, how about asking Grady or ask Namick instead of the moron which thought the whole idea of it up?

Money was why he thought it up. Money was why him and me always thought of any idea at all. In other words, Davie wasn't a lifeguard, but he had an idea of how to make money off of it. Grady and Namick were. Meaning, they were the ones in charge of the beach which was right across from Fascination. There's beach here and there's beach there, but this was the part of the beach where all of the big business got handled.

They were older individuals than Davie. They were the lifeguards, but it was Davie which was the swimmer! Okay, so here's the part you have been waiting for. Here is how it happened—that part, the Davie part.

Late August, early September, this is when the beach shuts down and the lifeguards put on the raffle. It's just a stunt, the raffle. It really isn't a one hundred percent thing, just to begin with. Let's face it, everybody knows what the story really is, which is to take care of the lifeguards as regards their tips and their gratuities for the summer. In other words, this is what they get extra, seeing as how they get next to nothing regular.

Do you see what I am saying? So there is this raffle which really is not a raffle. I mean, a raffle is just what they call it. Okay, it's like camisole, right? It gets called that. Except it's really the thing with the laces.

So to make a long story short, the prize is a bottle of liquor. So maybe it is worth, you know, let's say five dollars. Whereas what does a ticket go for? Let's say double.

Okay, actual figures I can't give you. But let's not forget, we are talking a different day and age. Some things you can wait for them to come back, but some things, I'm sorry, what's the percentage in waiting?

Number one, Davie gets the bottle from the samples.

Remember the samples? So if Davie gets the bottle, then he gets a cut on the take from the tickets. But this is just number one. Meaning, there are certain other factors! But let's just say money is the first and foremost of all of the factors. Didn't I tell you it always is?

We'll put it this way. I am pulling down thirty-five from Fascination. Whereas Davie is maybe getting probably plus this from his dancing lessons. So this is what the situation is as regards the household economics. Go ahead and add in her forty-five from McClellan's or Woolworth's or wherever, you've got all told something to think twice about when the summer is going to be over.

This is when she says we better start thinking about where we are turning next for extra, seeing as how she has done all of the waiting on the colored hand and foot she is ever going to, end of discussion, period.

I can understand this, her saying what the story was. On the other hand, this is not the policy I myself practice. I say, the less my own particular household knows, the better for all parties! Let's face it, I am making reference to T.C. and her outbursts. With this in mind, here is the answer. T.C. already is dealing enough with her nervous tension.

Here is my analysis. There is too much pressure to begin with! So if you start talking certain factors, what happens to the pressure? You see what I am saying?

I say this is no way to deal with the nature of the situation. I say dissemination of information only does what to the pressure? Whereas if it is T.C.'s outbursts which are the question, the best policy for us is not to make mention.

Do you see the thinking behind my thinking? Because this is what it is, take it or leave it.

Dissemination.

Like this. "Dissemination."

But don't waste your breath and ask me which number it was when I did it. Time out! Did I say something about a fat one where these bubble things keep coming out bubbling out around Paki? So did I or didn't I? Because I don't want to forget to tell you about that one. A real tubby! What was she doing with a job as a messenger? Hey, she's a messenger and she's walking her bicycle! Like she wants you to think it's because her tire is flat, but I say was it?

Forget it. I don't have time to take it up now. Except here's the thing. How do we pin down what it was coming bubbling from? Like a tumor couldn't do that, could it? Unless there is this type you can get which gas gets in it. I don't know. I guess this is one for the experts.

We don't have time for it now anyway. You think Norman is just sitting there twiddling his thumbs down there in Brooklyn? Do I have to remind present company what makes a bad situation worse and the fact that I already did it? Let's face it, there has been too much dissemination of information, as it goes without saying!

So getting back to the discussion of the raffle, which is the one we were already involved in. So with this in mind, reviewing the facts so far, the raffle is a phony, true or false?

Granted, it costs you ten to take a chance on something you only get half as much for. Whereas chances meanwhile are you won't get even this much to begin with. So Davie says this is where you have to have your rescue. On the other hand, I hear you say to me "What's the rescue?"

Okay, fair enough. This is a perfectly legitimate question.

So let's say for argument's sake, a certain somebody goes in the water. Let's also say this certain somebody goes out where it's too far out for his own good. So then the next thing is this individual starts drowning. He is screaming, "I am drowning!" So then the people in the public scream too. They scream, "Lifeguard, lifeguard, an individual is drowning!" So do you follow this mental picture?

Grady and Namick are ready and waiting! Don't kid yourself, they know from the word go the whole deal is a setup. Is anybody really drowning? Hey, forget it! It's just a patsy! It's just the individual they get to go along with the setup. So this is how come they look so good when they go out to get him out. You see what I am saying?

They go in and they look good and they go out and go get the patsy out!

Hey, the thing is to, you know, to do it up brown. The thing is to sell tickets! Whereas what is Davie's cut going to be for getting the sample and also thinking up the rescue?

The answer is a piece of the action, but this is only depending on things.

So you say to me, "Depending on what things?"

The answer is only if Davie also gets the patsy.

I say, "You be the patsy. It's your idea."

But Davie says to me he can't be because the people in the public know he is a swimmer!

SO LIKE I SAID, WASN'T THE WHOLE THING of it the money? Don't kid yourself, ask anybody. Meanwhile, the next thing you know, it's the Sunday in question because this is the last Sunday of the season. Whereas what does the city put up the night beforehand? The answer is a sign which says NO SWIMMING. Do you see what I'm saying? In other words, yours truly comes out and he sees it says NO SWIMMING. But meanwhile a certain someone came with him. Hey, are you kidding? You think I was going to let Janet Rose go get the wrong impression of me? Listen, I know I don't have to tell you! So I have got my trunks, but before I can get them on, you-know-who gets down on her knees back behind Fascination with me and gives me a big send-off with a, you know, with a French-off.

Listen, I'll be honest with you, the water looked to yours truly like it was getting beaten with an eggbeater!

I don't know, I have this crazy feeling like they are all of them waiting. You know what my theory is? They really are! Not just Janet Rose but everybody! They are waiting for somebody to come along and be the one to do something. Hey, for what it's worth, I'll give you my analysis—which is if somebody didn't, they'd wait till somebody did!

So I go past her where she's sitting on her blanket and I

say, "This is for Mr. and Mrs. First-Nighter." Then I get to the lifeguard station, and I say, "Get ready." But they don't say anything. Grady, I don't have to tell you, he is up on his chair per usual. Whereas Namick is on the catamaran flopping around his whistle. As regards Davie, I don't know, he must have been somewhere even if yours truly couldn't see him.

Hey, don't forget what's Everett's favorite icebreaker—"Everybody's got to be someplace."

You know what? I think it was his best one.

"You ready?" I said. "I am going in."

Grady says, "Hey, asshole, can't you read?"

Namick says, "Get the fuck away from here, kid—don't you see the deal is off?"

I say, "It's okay. We need the extra money."

Grady says, "Will somebody shut him up?"

I'll be honest with you. What if I did not see their sunglasses and the zinc salve on their noses? So then I look at the ocean. But it wasn't a thing you could look at either. This is when everything gets to be different. Because now all yours truly is doing is running. Whereas when you do it, this is all you can think about on account of the sand seeing you going. Hey, let's put it this way. It's like guess who just jumped into the worst thing a person could ever jump into. Listen, I won't kid you. I made maybe just yards tops when I already can see it is a foregone conclusion. It's like yours truly jumped and can't jump back. You know what? You know what is going through a certain person's head? The answer is the sky reached down and really, you know, did it!

I was screaming. But it's just bubbles. So I say to myself, "Keep breathing." But then I can't remember what I said. I mean, one minute you are running and you are thinking about who is watching and what. Whereas the next minute you're drowning and they can't even see you do it because they can't even see over the waves!

It's just yards in and there's no bottom. It's a fact and you can check it! Then the first backwash hits me and that's that. The beach is where? I can't see over the water to see it! But I don't know. Maybe I was facing in the wrong direction. Here's something. I can't even see the water I'm in! I just keep smacking at it and trying to catch a breath. But here is when another wave gets me on its way back— and when this one is through with me, hey, I am out past where the jetty is, okay?

But everybody's got to be someplace, right?

Listen, don't make me have to tell you, yours truly was praying. You know what? I was praying to Buddy Brown! No, forget it, this was not one hundred percent. What I was really doing was thinking something instead. Which is that my dad will come back when they tell him I'm dead—and when I am, won't I have to see Buddy Brown?

It's Namick and Grady who pull me out. Except I never see them until they're doing it. I don't even feel them yanking my hair. In other words, I thought it was the water which was, even though it's the two of them and the catamaran is knocking me in my head and my hair hurts and my crotch does because Grady has me by the trunks.

I'll be honest with you. I was crying. I was crying and screaming and making no sense. You know what I screamed? I screamed, "Where's Davie!" I was screaming, "Where's Davie!" Yours truly was screaming, "Davie made me do it, I swear it, I swear!"

What a moron brother!

I just thought of something. I mean, let's say you make one up. In other words, for argument's sake, you make a brother up. Fair enough. Now here is what I just thought of. Which is that if you stopped to make one up, could you make one up that was as big a moron as that one was?

On the other hand, God paid him back. But do me a favor and don't put this analysis in the book. Just between you, me, and the lamppost, the whole theory should have stayed under my hat. Am I right or am I right?

Here's something—we call it *The Old Maestro* instead of *Fascination*. So you tell me, is a certain somebody cooking with gas or is a certain somebody cooking with gas?

Meanwhile, it goes without saying, you're fifteen and you say things. So let's just say I said things to a certain Janet Rose! Meaning, it's after I get to Gotham with her and her mother. Whereas the next day Janet R. has to go to school to you-know-where. I don't have to tell you, with a thing like this you start thinking out loud. I mean, one thing leads to another, right? So before you know it, you are talking to your true love about your philosophies. Okay, so there I am in Gotham and the leaves are changing color. Number two, I don't have to remind you guess who has also been through the proverbial mill in her own right! So we are talking to each other and telling each other what our philosophies are—fathers and so forth and everything changing and the meaning of life and so on. Let's face it, Janet R. and yours truly could have written the book—fathers gone, mothers going crazy, this, that, and the other. So this is when I say to her, "Here is something I can't tell anybody."

She says, "Tell me."

So I say, "God punished him for what he did to Buddy."

She says, "Who?"

So I say, "My brother."

So Janet R. says, "A brother named Buddy? That's a nice name, a brother named Buddy."

HEY, THAT'S WHAT HE SAID! Not *yes sir, yes sir, yes sir*—but *yowsah, yowsah, yowsah!*

Oh, Mr. Capote, Mr. Capote, I got it! I got it! The Old Maestro said *yowsah, yowsah, yowsah.*

Hotdog! I told you it was coming back!

This is Ben Bernie, ladies and gentlemen, and all the lads in the band, wishing you a bit of pleasant dreams, a bit of a tweet-tweet, a fond cheerio from the Old Maestro, yowsah, yowsah, yowsah.

It's coming, I knew it would! That's not it yet, not exactly as it was yet, but it will, it will!

Yowsah, yowsah, yowsah.

You see what the Old Maestro did? He took *yes sir, yes sir, yes sir* and made it *yowsah, yowsah, yowsah.* This is because the whole thing of it with Ben Bernie was for Ben Bernie to make it easy and sleepy and nice!

He said *dree yums.* You see what I mean? For *dreams,* when he said it, Ben Bernie said *dree yums.*

Oh God, it's nice.

It was so sleepy and nice. Just listen. See if it doesn't make you feel sleepy and nice. *This is the Old Maestro saying yowsah, yowsah, yowsah, au revoir, a fond cheerio, a bit of a tweet-tweet, and pleasant dree yums.* You see? Dree yums.

Not like today. I don't have to tell you what it is all like in this day and age. I should get down on my hands and knees and thank God that I am not in the show business of today.

Hey, let's face it, I don't envy you having to write bestsellers for the kind of people in the public today! The people of today wouldn't let you get to first base with something sleepy and nice. You take the classics like the ones you write. They don't mean a thing to the caliber of people which are going around in this day and age! Believe me, these individuals, they're not laying out good money for one Kansas family all inside of only one only house!

Don't kid yourself, everybody's got to keep up with the times! You blink your eyes, and there it goes, getting out in front of you, a ten-speed all the way! But, come on, you tell me, isn't this where yours truly and Paki come in?

Yowsah, yowsah, yowsah.

Tonight, for example. In other words, okay, *Newsline* comes on. So what is her top story, present company's latest bestseller or Paki's latest you-know-what?

Time out! It's time for a correction! Correction: It's Kathleen, not Catherine.

Can you believe it? I mean, it just suddenly dawned on me how I had it all balled up. It's Kathleen Campion on Channel 13. Meaning, the individual with hair like Janet R.'s—except if you think of Barbara Luddy's name, you get the same idea. Like the one of curly and pretty and brown.

Oh my God, as God is my judge! I mean, I just had this second thing with names!

Norman and Truman! Truman and Norman!

Do you see what I am saying?

It just hit me like a ton of bricks where the both of them have the same word in it! Whereas guess which one it is! Hey, is this one for the books, or is this one for the books?

It's like everything's the same thing! It's like the things with the laces is Buddy Brown, whereas Ben Bernie is what it is when they say, "Drink it and fall asleep."

I don't know. You think there is something in this? Or is this just yours truly making mountains out of molehills all over again? Hey, let's not kid ourselves, there is something in everything, you name it!

For instance, there is something in the air, true or false? In a pica, true or false? In a minute, true or false?

Listen to this. Here are some quotes of her.

"Let's not and say we did."

"Hold the phone."

"Lord, Lord."

The boy can tell you how long a pica is. Or a minute.

One thing I can tell you, T.C. said he would. In other words, you can't stop a boy from racing—this is T.C.'s thinking and this is what she said. But it goes without saying, he didn't have a chance! Seven watts to the good, but seven gears underpowered! Let's be honest with each other, a girl and a colored on top of it!

For what it's worth, here is my personal analysis.

This is why the boy is not riding it on Sundays anymore! On the other hand, he says it's the streets. Meaning, you never know what's out there, bodily harm just to begin with!

T.C. says he needs the air. But I say there is plenty of it upstairs. Listen, I am the one which breathes easier when guess who is safe and sound you-know-where.

I mean, let's not forget when yours truly was seven and we moved to the other house. I knew what could happen when you went outside in the air! And don't kid yourself, it did! Just for openers, they kept building more houses. Am I right or am I right? But even when they got them finished, was there or wasn't there one they never did?

Hey, I guess I don't have to tell you which one that one is!

It was November, or it was March. It was a month like when the weather was the way it is in a month when everything gets muddy and dark. Let's face it, any way you looked at it, the new block was mostly always muddy and dark. Meaning, it just had this type of a look to it. To my mind, it looked all dug up! To my mind, it looked to me like they could never make up their mind what for them to do with it, even if they really did!

You know what? It was mud instead of grass!

The other thing is, the boys were new just the way the houses were. Davie was the only one which wasn't. But would Davie make sense and stay inside and play? He went out. He was out there in it all of the time and came in with mud on him all of the time! Look at this—mud on his hair! So you tell me, can you be a picture-book boy with mud on your hair? Listen, do me a favor and don't make me laugh!

I am talking about the new block. You don't understand what it means when I talk about the new block. Don't you see that I was seven? Hey, you want to know something? Pulmotor. So the thing is this, did I have to get it off of any Word-a-Day calendar? Believe me, everybody has to live and learn! Even a famous celebrity does!

Listen, I respect your second-rater as much as the next one does. But I am here to tell you, it is going to take more than some second-rater to pull a thing like this together. With all due respect, who else but present company could handle a subject on this order? You know what? I say Norman knew he couldn't! This is my personal analysis. Face facts. Norman could see how this was way over his head! The block, for instance. In other words, when it comes to telling about the block, I'm serious, it is going to take a genius to do it!

Balloon! That's what you call those fat tires—balloon tires! Hey, look at that. I mean, the thing of it is, I was trying to remember the type of tires which the messenger was acting like they were going flat. Let's not kid ourselves, it was all (joke) in her head, ha ha.

You see? I guarantee you, there is nothing which does not come back. Balloon is just another example! Believe me, you are never going to have to say to me, "And then what happened?" Where yours truly is concerned, don't worry, it is all coming back to me. I know what happened next and then the next thing after that!

So one wasn't enough of an example? So here is another one if you want proof. The puddle! I even remember my shoe when I stepped in the puddle. I even hear the ice when I stepped and it broke. But let us not sit here and forget who pulled me! I mean, if she didn't, would we have to turn around and go home?

Here are some other things. Fourteenth Street! How about the pizza maker when he came out of the doorway! Let's face it, it's things like these. It is your breath when you can't breathe. It is your breath when Janet Rose says, "Look in the mirror." It is your arm when Paki goes through the socket and then through the thing which is wrapped inside of there around the brain!

Your average individual, this kind of thing goes right over their head. Your average individual, all they want is the highlights, end of discussion, period. Individual, your average individual, listen, what's the percentage? Like the salesperson at May's when yours truly finally gets upstairs to ask them about a miracle.

Do you see what I am saying?

I was in a state. I was shaking like a leaf. I was green around the gills. I was a person which was just outside there where everything in the world was different!

I said, "Guess what I just saw."

He says to me, "What? Somebody get killed?"

You see what I mean? I mean, is this your average individual or isn't it? God is my witness, it makes me sick. Leaving present company and Janet R. out of it, wherever you turn it is just another average individual!

GOTHAM WAS THE NEXT BIG STEP. I just went with Janet R. when she went back to Gotham with her mother. I didn't go home after Davie went down to Davie Jones's locker—to use a certain manner of speaking.

Nobody said anything when yours truly got off of the catamaran. Nobody even looked at me in particular. Just think, all of those people in the public there, but aren't they all average? I mean, does anybody stop to think?

Forget it! Present company should not bother his little head about this, no kidding!

I was freezing. It was just like with the puddle. Whereas the difference was, that was just my foot! The thing of it is, there wasn't any reason for me to think about anything except to think about being cold. Here's something. I keep opening my mouth to yawn. I keep opening my mouth to get it open wide enough for me to get a good yawn.

To tell you the truth, I never took another look at the ocean. The next thing is, here comes Janet Rose. She says, "Baby." She puts her blanket around me. She says, "Oh, little baby." She says, "Let Mama come and take little baby and go get little baby's clothes."

It's like *yowsah, yowsah, yowsah*. Just to think of how she said it, it makes me want to sleep. Oh, Mr. Capote, I am so sleepy all of the time even if I can't really do it.

Should you ever send in your requesta—why, we'll sure try to do our besta—yowsah, yowsah, yowsah.

It's the truth. I won't kid you. It is so hard for me to sleep. But, hey, don't get the wrong impression! Believe me, it is not what I think you are thinking. It's just where all of my life I was a bad sleeper from the word go. Let's face it, I'm talking ancient history! But the thing of it was, everybody was always sleeping—whereas could a certain person? Granted, it made me sweaty, not being able to when they could. Hey, you know how it is, how you go from bad to worse? I mean, you go this way and that way and then back to this way again. Then you start hearing things in your ears. You hear this type of noise. But does anyone tell you what it is? I mean, it was the same differ-ence as the vacuum before she went to business. Well, what does dissemination of information get you? Like if you make reference, your average individual just laughs.

So yours truly just stayed awake with the radio by his bed. Meanwhile, I'm saying to myself if they hear it they are going to be really mad. Hey, forget it! They were always sleeping so they never heard a word!

He didn't say request. He said requesta. That's what the Old Maestro said! Just listen. He took request and what did he make it? He made it requesta! So stop and think a minute why he did it. The answer is just listen. Isn't request the wrong kind of word? I mean, it's like I said to you at the very beginning of this letter to you. It is all a question of the right word being in the right place. But the right one has to start out being the wrong one! Or maybe vice versa.

I don't know. It was a Ben Bernie thing.

Do you think this was because he was a bandleader? I have to think about it. Maybe it was because he led a band as a bandleader on the radio.

"Baby, baby, baby." This is what she said. All the way back to Fascination, that was Janet Rose's word. So what is your personal opinion of this? Did she start with the wrong one or did she start with the wrong one?

We went to the concession and got my clothes. We went from there to Janet R.'s hotel. We sat in the lobby. This is because this is what she said we had to do. She said we should not go up to you-know-where until her mother came back from wherever her mother was. But when she didn't, we went up the stairs to guess whose room.

Here's something.

Did you know this was another first for Mr. and Mrs. First-Nighter? In other words, we were in a room. And here's another one. I told her it was the same. Can you believe it? I said it was the hotel where Davie did his dancing! But who knows, maybe it was not. The thing is, it was hard to tell. I mean, yours truly was not seeing things as sharp as he is used to doing. It's like they took away the glass, so your eyes get full of dust. It is the same thing as when you look through the see-through ruler. You see what I am saying? It's like you either see the scale or you see the thing you're measuring. Forget it. It's like Peter and Paul. It's just like with requesta. You either see it or you don't. Let's just say I am in a chair next to a chest of drawers and Janet R. is saying, "Baby, baby, baby." But so far as a certain person goes, I do not do anything but, you know, just sit there.

You think it was an act or wasn't it? I mean, was I just doing this to look like I was a boy who couldn't do something, true or false? In my analysis, I think I was. But let's face it, who really ever really knows? Believe me, you think you yourself are the expert? Hey, let's not kid ourselves. In this department, not even a famous celebrity has got the last word nohow!

You want to hear the payoff? When I was a little boy, I

was always faking. You name it, my face, my voice! I even did it if nobody was there! Correction: Even if nobody was, things were—plus guess who was.

It could be for anything. It could be for the paper I am writing on. It could be for the ocean I was drowning in. How about for the chair or for the chest of drawers?

What I am saying is, you look this way or that way for things. It is not a question of only eyes. Ditto also goes for saying things and ears! Hey, you think this is a crackpot theory? Because maybe yours truly is all balled up with just some crackpot theory.

This is a personal opinion I just thought of.

Isn't everybody always doing just like I was?

I guarantee you, their faces are not the faces they let you look at. Take my word for it, they're not!

So think back to when I told you I couldn't fall asleep. So here's the thing! Sometimes I think it was only because I wanted the bed to see me not doing it! Plus the same goes for why I didn't run up the block when Buddy Brown fell. Pretty crazy, right? But the thing of it is, it's the same thing! I mean, I wanted the house I was in to see me sitting alone in it and being scared.

So you tell me. So which was I? Was I really scared or was I just scared for the good of the house? Take when I can't sleep—is it just so the bed will see a person which can't? I don't know. Except please do not put any of this in the book. Don't worry, yours truly has his reasons!

You take the people which come to you and they ask

you the three questions. You think they know the answers? Granted, they know the answers to the three questions. But let's face it, this is only because they were the same individuals which sat there and made them up!

Illaudable. How do you like this word? Now watch this. "Illaudable." Number which one on the list I can't tell you, because even a genius can't remember them all! But the thing is, you think the face she showed Paki was the real face she had? Hey, do me a favor and don't make me laugh! Face facts! It is just the face you put on so that you are putting on the one for a knife!

Like you take the one which Janet Rose put on for when the hairbrush was up her in her you-know-what. Whereas suppose you were watching her toes! Hey, or better yet, her you-know-what itself! You see what I am saying? Believe me, where your real story is is somewhere else!

Me, I say you're better off with the one which is made up. Number one, just imagine what it would be like if you had to be the other way all of the time. You know what? It would wear your face out! You would use it up! Fake faces are just this thing where Nature is helping you live a longer life! Like Scheindel Kalish, right? She makes believe she's Ann Shepherd, you know how much longer she keeps Scheindel Kalish in the ball game?

Listen, as one individual to another, take my advice. You let Nature take her course. She makes you a phony, sure, but look for whose good she is doing it for!

I'll bet you never thought about this before. Let's face it, nobody does. Meaning, look what happens when you think a thing all the way through! It comes out backwards! Take anything and keep on thinking it through. You know what you get? You get the backwards of what you started with when you first took.

Take me, for example. You name me the individual which is more perturbed when he is in the vicinity of some bodily harm. Whereas stop to think what yours truly is doing when he makes them stop and stare. You see how it comes out backwards? Hey, the whole thing of it is, be big about it. You get small, where's the room for all the contradictions which keep on getting inside of yourself? Like it or lump it, this is my philosophy in a nutshell.

On the other hand, you take the salesperson last Christmas, okay? In other words, I am making reference to the one which sold me the three-speed and which also tried to sell yours truly this bill of goods about no written warranty and so forth and so on. I mean, the thing of it is, what did he want to know? "Did anybody get killed?" End of discussion, period! But I ask you, isn't this the type of thinking you get when you don't think a thing through?

Because nobody got killed! But do I have to tell present company this is what makes it worse than if somebody did? Hey, it really makes you want to vomit, an individual with this kind of thinking.

Listen, I'll give you another example.

T.C. and yours truly have this tiff, okay? It is the usual thing. Long story short, it's household economics or it's the boy's educational experiences, whatever. So the thing is, it's an outburst, but what about my tongue? Meaning, it was a Thursday after a Wednesday and I figure my tongue has had enough. For the good of all concerned, I say to myself the thing is for me to make myself scarce. Be it as it may that this it is not my regular custom, yours truly takes his leave of the premises, okay? Listen, I promise you, for me the marriage vows are the marriage vows irregardless. Which I say goes double on Sunday! But let's be honest with each other, it was a Thursday after a Wednesday and I just could not sit here anymore and keep taking it.

Listen, when T.C. is in a state, T.C. is in a state. So even if you talk yourself blue in the face, there is only one way for yours truly to make amends. Besides, isn't you-know-who hearing every word of this particular outburst? Hey, forget it! They can hear it in the Hamptons, enough said?

I say, "Sweetheart, little pitchers have big ears."

But does T.C. take the hint? So I say to myself the way they used to say on the radio, "It is time for me to take a powder." Whereas the next thing I know, I'm over by the river and I see a certain someone and a certain someone sees me. So in words of one syllable, we take a little walk together over to her place together.

Believe me, it's like I told you, I still have my looks. Listen, even if I don't have all of them, I still have some of them, whatever Janet R. said irregardless!

She wasn't much. One thing is, she gets herself so tanked up with your alcoholic beverage, when it comes time for what is on the agenda, she's just meat. But is this the reason I made mention of this? Far from it. Here is the reason I raised the subject for present company to begin with. Which is when later on she comes in and, you know, guess where gets busy shaving!

Sit tight. This is the mental picture.

It's dark out, okay? So yours truly is getting ready to get out of there and get back to you-know-where. But before I can go, I notice as to how guess who should probably use this individual's place to empty out my water. So I am sitting there, right? I mean, this is the way I do it, as I already told you. When in she comes and starts putting the stuff on her and getting out her razor!

I'll be honest with you, even this was good. In other words, it's watching people in the public do the things they do when you are not supposed to be there! And I don't have to tell you, this is how she is acting—like I am definitely not, end of discussion, period.

First thing she goes is, "How come you do it like that? You got something busted or something?"

I go, "It's quieter. I like it better quieter."

She goes, "Yeah, yeah, honey, something busted—don't worry about it."

She keeps on getting on her this shaving stuff all over her, getting everything all covered.

Next thing she goes is, "Jesus, honey, make room—I ain't got all night."

This is when she puts her foot up. In other words, on

the seat! I mean, her toes right there in the middle of where yours truly is sitting doing his business. So then she like wobbles her knee back and forth. It is like she is checking for the best spot to get the razor started. It is like the boy who backed up into the coat rack. It is like here is where you are, so where do you go from here? Meaning, everybody's got to be someplace, right?

Meanwhile, here is the thing. There is this view which yours truly is getting of her of her privates on account of her flopping her knee around on account of her shaving! Hey, it's her trying to get to the harder to get to places which is when I even can see her privates changing!

You don't understand. It's not seeing them which counts. Doesn't it go without saying you can always see one of them when you want to? T.C.'s, for instance, she lets me look at hers, doesn't she? Whereas this is the whole thing of it! If they let you, then you never see what's secret! Whereas the thing of it with the one which was shaving was seeing it when there is something going on which has nothing to do with you seeing it! You see what I am saying? I mean, you tell me, do I have a theory here or do I have a theory here? Let's face it, this is something to really stop and think about!

You know how when you shave your face. You know how when you do, you keep moving it to get to another part of it. So get this. It is the same way with one of them! Meaning, a certain person is turning this way and that way to get to all of the places. She pulls the skin and pushes it, doing some of all these little things to it, her toes meanwhile doing some of their own things in the bargain. Whereas each little thing brings her you-know-what into play in a new way—and guess who can see every iota of the whole deal! I mean, here is the mental picture. Her privates are acting like yours truly is not even there. And even if they really know I am, they are showing me the things you only show when you want for somebody to think you are, you know, showing secrets!

You see the thing I'm saying? It's like "Somebody get killed?" In other words, the thing which was really something wasn't the thing when she was meat. It was the thing when she put her foot up on the toilet seat! But is this the thing your average individual goes out of their way for them to hear about? Don't kid yourself, all they want to know is did somebody get killed! Believe me, they don't even ask you, "How come they threw paper?"

The man at May's, for instance, did he pay any attention after yours truly said nobody did?

NOW HERE'S ANOTHER THING, and it's the same night as the first thing. I get my clothes back on and follow up with Paki per usual. Maybe *iota,* maybe *scintilla.* I think it was the *iota* one, but do not hold me to it. But for argument's sake, we'll just say this is what I said. "Iota."

The streets are empty going home. Which is the part

where this new thing comes in. So when this wave hits, it's just the two of these individuals. I don't have to tell you I am making reference to the pizza maker and the other one. Like a person in your circle would spot this other one right off. I mean, the way he is tall and has a sport coat and the type of hair. In my analysis, this is how your top bank officer looks when he is not at his branch.

So long story short, yours truly is proceeding with all due caution. For example, you walk on the curb and you watch the doorways which keep coming up on the one side you've got to watch. In other words, it is times like these when you have got to get all of the way up on them. I mean, on the toes in the corners of your eyes. Also, don't think I am not listening for what could be moving in at me from behind. Let's face it, a wave can come at you from anywhere, not to mention from behind. Which is just what yours truly is thinking about when, bingo, here it comes! But it's just two of these individuals, the pizza maker and the tall one in the sport coat.

Hey, don't kid yourself, maybe it's just the two of them, but it was the fastest wave of all! Where it starts from is from the door of the pizza place and from there it goes like ripping across the sidewalk, but no noise, not any noise! Except for this jingling sound.

Like this. Jingle, jingle, jingle.

See if you can see this, the thing going across right in front of me. Number one, it comes out from the door of the pizza place. Number two, it goes across the sidewalk right in front of yours truly. Number three, it comes to a stop in the middle of the street, which is First Avenue, just by way of giving you the whole thing of the way guess who sees it. First, there's the pizza maker, which is this very wide but very short individual in like a candy-stripe shirt. So this is the first one, who has a hold of the tall one. He has him in a hold around the, you know, the waist. I mean, you tell me. Isn't the waist a funny-looking place for you to have a hold of someone? Don't kid yourself, it is! So that's how the short one's got him and he is running with him into the middle of the street. But then when he gets him there, he lets go and climbs and jumps. Do you see what I am saying? The one in the candy-stripe shirt? In other words, he can't hit the other one where he wants to hit him unless he climbs up to reach it or stands there and jumps! So he climbs! So he jumps! And this is where more of this jingle, jingle, jingle is involved.

Also the smacks you hear when the pizza maker smacks this individual on the head!

Up there, all of the way up. Right up there on the top! Smack, smack, smack.

It's got the sport coat all bunched up.

Did I tell you there is flour all over them? It's on their faces! So you see how this makes the eyes stick out? Not to mention the mouth of the same individual when he opens it up. But here's the point. There is nothing like any noise which comes out! I mean, all you hear is the pizza maker jumping and the smacks. And way off, this jingle like.

Here is something else. The individual who is so tall is not doing anything but stand there. He just stands there letting the other individual jump up. To my way of thinking, this is the worst part. Except for the jingle, jingle, jingle. This and the way their faces are all powdery all over and there is nothing else for you to hear except the smacks.

Listen to this. It is the same thing as the time when yours truly gets off the catamaran. Meaning, as regards me, the people in the public, they were probably screaming, but it was quiet. All there is is this jingling when the pizza maker jumps and the tall fellow just stands there and lets him hit him on the head. Right on the top of it. Up here in the middle of the top—smack, smack, smack. But it is like there is no noise even though there is! I can't explain it. It's like the things you hear don't go with the things you see. Let's face it, it's floppy and also gooey. Here is my analysis for what it is worth—it is always floppy and gooey. But both of them at once! Like the pizza maker's shoes when he is climbing up! Or how the sport coat of the other individual is all bunched up! So this is the floppy part, just the way it was when the boy with the knife slips on the ice with the knife and then gets all balled up in the coats on the coat rack. So this is gooey and floppy, except both things at once!

Hey, forget it. You just have to go see it like you went and saw those boys in Kansas.

The whole deal was what? Seconds? In other words, from start to finish, it's like Simon's, in and out! The wave comes! The wave goes! The pizza maker is back in his place, whereas the other individual is right where the pizza maker left him standing in the street. So this is when it looks the gooiest, the one with the nice hair just standing there with his mouth open not even crying or even screaming but just with powder, or powdery.

Hey, did anybody get killed?

Don't they see it's worse than that? The pizza maker climbed up on him and hit him on the head! Sometimes he had to jump and he was wearing a candy-stripe shirt! And their faces, so white! Plus the tall one letting him do it like he is something you are supposed to jump up and climb up on!

The people in the public! All they want to know is did anybody get killed! But do they care about the jingle, jingle, jingle? Hey, don't make me laugh. Like with the salesperson at May's, this is what is wrong with your people of today! All they know is did anybody get killed. But you go and give them something good, don't waste your breath, you won't even get to first base! They would sit there and say to you, "Jingle, jingle, jingle—so what's that?"

You know what? It just breaks my heart how you only have a handful of individuals which know what the story is. But so there you go—the people in the public and you and me. I mean, that's the deal right there. The pizza maker goes back in and the other one keeps standing there in the middle of the street, whereas yours truly runs all of the way home because not to would be crazy.

Listen, I have to tell you something. I said to myself, "I better run before this individual in the street sees me." In other words, look at it this way. Suppose you are there watching and Buddy Brown turns around and looks up at you when he is already halfway down? You see what I am saying? Meaning, he is halfway down through where the chimney is going to go, but then he looks up and sees you looking down at him when you are looking down! So if this happened, then what? Which is what I keep on trying to tell you!

This is why yours truly runs all of the way home. It's also why it is a piece of cake when I get there. Meaning, there is something to tell T.C. before she can start asking guess who about something else. Like for instance, what was a certain person doing before he got good and ready to come home like a decent citizen? Well, listen—long story short, she isn't even a little bit interested anyway. She just says, "Lord, Lord, look at what the cat dragged in," and goes back to watching something. I don't know. Maybe it was probably *Charlie's Angels*. Come on, if it is not Channel 13, then it is not Channel 13!

I'll be honest with you, I went ahead with it anyway. I mean, the situation with my tongue irregardless. I figure make amends and be done with it! Look, in sickness or in health, enough said? So I do the front until she says you-know-what, and then she rolls over and gets her finger down there to get herself to her finish, it standing to reason yours truly is meanwhile going to do the back as good as it is humanly possible for me to under the circumstances.

This is what the thing of it is. It's not that I am just doing my duty. Because the facts are the facts and you can't get around them! Meaning, when it comes to T.C., the facts are I love her! On the other hand, I won't kid you. When they come and visit wherever they've got me, Janet R. gets in first! Even if it's T.C. which is the official missus!

HEY, I CAN TALK TO YOU LIKE THIS, true or false? I mean, it's okay if the conversation gets a little off-color? Norman you couldn't warm up to in this particular department. I'm here to tell you, with Norman you always had this feeling you better not let your hair down. Let's face it, I kept trying to. But in my personal opinion, you couldn't get close to the man if you stood on your left ear to do it! My theory is this. As soon as I opened up my mouth to him about this, that, and the other, it comes to me that he is saying to himself I am getting lower and lower in his eyes. To tell you the truth, I think he holds it against me. Meaning, doing T.C. both sides. But I don't know. Maybe this is just my thinking and I am wrong to point a finger.

Listen, when it comes to thinking, don't think you can't go overboard! I mean, strictly for the sake of argument, some thoughts you are better off without! Like would I be wide awake all night if I thought of something else? On the other hand, the answer is what? In other words, you are in the, you know, the bed. So doesn't it make sense the bed is what you are thinking of? Am I right or am I right?

Illaudable. This will make you laugh. It's crazy, but I am not ashamed to tell you. It sounds to me like it means something about hair, like about hair being gentle and soft and so on and so forth. So here is the thing. Going back to before I saw Janet R.'s you-know-what, that's what yours truly thought! You see what I am saying? I mean, I used to think girls would be like this if you got a look at their privates. I mean, like it sounds when you say illaudable! Hey, but I was all wet from the word go, true or false? I mean, you take Sylvia Berman's, granted, it was sort of. But so far as Janet R.'s mother's or Janet R.'s, it was nothing on this order, not to mention the nature of the situation as regards to T.C.'s herself. On the other hand, T.C.'s is light in color and there is not overly much of it. Hey, here's something. You look at T.C.'s and you can almost see her Devil's you-know-what. I mean, even if she is just standing there, you can almost. No kidding, I'm serious.

All right, I won't lie to you. Let's face it, you probably would have caught me at it anyway. In other words, the reason I made reference to this is I was trying to see if I could get another boner! I mean, I was thinking about yours truly and Janet Rose in Janet Rose's mother's hotel room. So one thing leads to another, and the next thing you know, I am sitting here thinking about Janet Rose in her bathing suit with the hairs you-know-where sticking out of it a little bit! So I said to myself, "Look out, you are going to get another boner!"

Granted, it was just a handful of them. But I don't have to tell you this was another first for a certain person, seeing the hairs of the you-know-what of my beloved Janet Rose!

But getting back to the situation, I'll put it this way. This is how I went away. I did not take anything but the clothes I had at Fascination. Plus the money they owed me—don't forget the money!

I tried to go to sleep in the cellar of the hotel. Naturally, yours truly is making reference to the night before I went away to Gotham with Janet Rose and her mother. But I could not do it. Number one, I knew I was supposed to be thinking about Davie. But all I could do was think about going to Gotham and the hairs of her you-know-what. I kept thinking what it would look like if you could see all of them. Listen, I'll be honest with you, I kept thinking if I would ever get to have a look at Janet Rose's privates.

Number two, it was the cellar. Meaning, wasn't this the cellar of the Traymore or of the Broadmoor or of the Shelburne or whatever? So I don't have to tell you it probably was where Davie was always giving his lessons when he was dancing! On the other hand, when was a certain person ever a sleeper?

I said to myself, "Somebody should call her up and tell her." I thought of all of the different things to say to her.

Like this. "Lady, are you the mother of the boy who pushed Buddy Brown?" "Lady, did you ever stop to think before you moved?" "Lady, you had to move, but did you have to leave a certain hassock behind?" "Lady, want to see how long a minute is?" "Lady, it's his own fault the moron drowned."

Listen, you can see it for yourself! Her with her white shoes on her, except they never really were because they were filthy dirty even the day she came home with them! What other individual had shoes like that? Special shoes for special feet which have to have special support? So you tell me! You think a person with feet like that was really a dancer, true or false? Hey, do me a favor and don't make me laugh! She said they were dancing. But I say she had veins popping out! They came out of the closet and a certain individual had veins popping out!

Hey, I just thought of something. *Did you ever see a lassie go this way and that way and this way and that way?* It really makes you think, you know? I mean, me seeing her standing around in her shoes for Davie to come home and for me to show up. But instead it is somebody which says, "Lady, he's dead," or "Lady, he come and got his money and left."

I was on my way to Gotham! This was the thing of it and the rest was nothing nohow! Janet Rose said it was the answer to our prayers—Mr. and Mrs. First-Nighter! She said here is the way for us to think about it, and this is the way I did! She said it is just Nature taking its course!

I am here to tell you, Janet Rose was smart.

Let's put it this way, I had twenty dollars, minus what it cost me for the two frozen custards which yours truly got. You're laughing. But this was good money in that day and age irregardless of what your circle was!

Like you take like your inch and your pica. Okay, your inch is bigger, but what happens when you put your inch next to your mile? You see what I mean? You're not laughing so much now, are you? Whereas, granted, an inch is plenty when it only takes how many of them to get through your eyeball and jab you in your you-know-what! Hey, that's as far as anything ever has to get! I mean, how much farther can anybody ever go than a foreign object in your brain?

Time out. I looked it up. The boy has this book, so I took a look. Here is what happens according to the experts. The optic chiasm! It gets into something called that! And that's just for openers, right? Is this one for the books or is this one for the books? Check it out! *Your Body and What Is in It.* Whereas they don't give the name of the author, but big deal, what's the diff? I don't have to tell you, whoever this individual is, they are not some famous celebrity eating any fabulous lunches at your fabulous, you know, C.B. I mean, *Your Body and What Is in It*, did you ever hear of a title with less of a punch to it than that?

Where's your Authorized? Or even your Mutual?

Forget it!

Twenty-three optic chiasms!

And guess what's in back of all twenty-three of them once Paki goes and gets enough picas in!

Hey, talk about your *Fascination*, right? Or how about your, you know, your title like *The Old Maestro*?

"Red Dog, Red Dog—please call in, please!"

Listen to this. You know what he's got in his pocket down there under the seven-watter?

A dollar!

End of discussion, period.

Okay, you can laugh your head off over that one, but this is what he's got. And the reason why is this.

It is another one of yours truly's major rules!

So okay, so here's the deal. There are these two major rules yours truly inherited from his father, that one and the one about brown paper. Like this—"Always have a dollar in your pocket!" "Don't ever go anywhere without a dollar in your pocket!" "Whatever happens, have a dollar in your pocket!"

Hey, the jingling! The jingle, jingle, jingle! Hold the phone! You think what he had was lots of change as far as having a dollar in his pocket?

Lord, Lord, all it takes is waiting till it's ready to come, yowsah, yowsah, yowsah. I mean, you tell me—let's say yours truly stayed right there in the Plymouth. In other words, strictly for argument's sake, let's just say this is what he did. You see how there is all the diff? Whereas just picture me in Janet Rose's mother's car, jumping up and down every minute. You think I could sit still for two seconds? Hey, a certain person knows he was supposed to be a boy with a dead brother, but I'll be honest with you. So far as I was concerned, guess who was an individual on the way to Gotham!

It made me lean forward. It made me look around. It made me ask Janet Rose's mother lots of questions.

She says, "Where do we drop you?"

I say, "I don't know. You do what your heart tells you."

Janet Rose says, "He can decide when we get there." She says, "We'll go home and he can decide from there."

So this is how yours truly gets to live there. In other words, you just had to leave a thing to Janet Rose. You left it to her, whatever it was, and watch out, Janet R. took care of it from there, don't worry.

I HELPED THEM UP WITH THEIR STUFF. By the time suppertime came, I was still there and they said for me to stay. The mother gave me a plate. We ate at a table in the kitchen. I'm not going to kid you, it wasn't such a wonderful place. But it was much nicer than the one I'd come from, not to mention the one where I and mine are in housekeeping keeping residence as of now.

Did I say her father did something in the dress business? So this is my analysis, dresses pay off better than liquor. Even if he didn't live there either, just the way a certain somebody else's father didn't, you could see this was the case.

After supper we go sit in the living room. It's like being a family, isn't it? The mother keeps asking what is to be done with me, whereas Janet R. keeps saying the thing is to let Nature take its course. Meanwhile, here is the thing I notice. Which is the mother keeps drinking from a glass. I loved it in the room. I loved it, just listening. I loved it, just sitting watching their mouths doing these different things. Hey, and let's not forget Janet Rose's. Because a certain person's mind keeps thinking to myself, "That's the mouth which does it to your privates!"

I didn't do any of the talking. I liked it better with her talking. Here's what she said. She says the truth is I was running away. She says I had every reason in the world to. She tells her what they are. But let's face it, they aren't anything I ever thought of before. To make a long story short, I think I stopped listening. I don't think the mother was either. Here's why. She gets up in the middle of it and just goes off. She gets the bottle she has been pouring out of and just, you know, just goes off.

This is when Janet R. makes a place for me on the sofa. It is just a blanket and a pillow. But I say how she did it was so nice, so nice. Then she says for me to lie still—that when it is all right for her to, she will come get me.

I want to be aboveboard with you. Mr. Capote. This was the greatest night of a certain person's life! I say this to you in all honesty—even though I did not see anything. But there was nakedness! Let's face it, we were afraid to turn on the light. On the other hand, you-know-who took her nightie off. Or maybe it was her pajamas. I don't know. It could have been just the top.

I won't kid you, I was too excited. We were naked lying down. She let me hold her. She said I could not touch her places but I could hold her if I want. She said, "Baby, baby, baby." She said it was okay for me to hold her but not for there to be any touching anywhere near any of her privates.

It was wonderful!

It was the most wonderful thing there was!

We had to just whisper. We whispered how I loved her and that she was my beloved. I said that we were Mr. and Mrs. First-Nighter. She said, "Oh, baby, am I making it hard for you?" She said, "Baby, baby, baby, look how hard this makes it get for you!"

Hey, you guessed it! I just made myself get a big boner again. But to tell you the truth, it is like trying to remember what Ben Bernie said. One minute you have it, one minute you don't! I mean, let's be frank. At this stage of the game, what is the point in us not being honest together? A certain somebody can't be expected to remember everything! You take the one whose eyeball was like a cork stuck in a toilet. When you remember a thing like this, it is hard for you to remember everything else!

Enough said? I mean, at this time of the night, let's not kid ourselves! Rome wasn't built in a day, you know? Besides, the other thing is I'm getting tired! Did I tell you

I'm tired? God is my judge, I am! My arm, my hand, my fingers, not to mention my you-know-what from sitting on it from the beginning of this here in the kitchen like this!

Okay, the one with the muck which comes out, I'm trying to think. Was she *illaudable* or was she *amentia?* Because I know it wasn't the colored in the can! Because with the colored in the can there wasn't any word at all. Only, hey, don't think that one was such a picnic either!

Listen, I wasn't born yesterday, you know! In other words, you don't have to send me a telegram, okay? Believe me, nobody has to tell me nothing nohow. I guarantee you, I know as well as the next one I don't deserve any medals, do I? In all humility, you should get your head examined if this is what you think I think!

You think I'm cut out for this kind of thing? You think a thing like this comes easy to an individual of my type? You think when I am lying there my first night with Janet Rose yours truly is thinking how in thirty-odd years a certain person is going to have to sit in his kitchen with Paki in his pocket, which God forbid I don't get sharpened before certain people just so happen to wake up? You think anybody ever stops to think a thing like this? Don't flatter yourself, we all got a lot to learn! That's all I can say. Live and learn, believe me, this is the whole thing of it right there!

You know what I was thinking then and there? Yours truly was thinking here I am naked with a certain somebody in Gotham and a grown-up could walk in any minute! I was thinking look at all of the things which are happening to a certain individual and what is going to be the next thing which does?

I said, "Where would there be for me without you? You are my beloved," I said.

She said, "Hush, baby, hush."

She got down between my legs. She did it with her mouth. She did it right up until the time you almost go ahead and have your finish, and then she took it out. She says, "Baby, baby, baby." Then she puts it back. Then she takes it out. She says, "Baby, baby, baby."

It went on and on. It was better than anything there ever was. It was the best thing which ever happened to me until the next thing which Janet Rose did!

She says, "Hush, baby," and gets up off the bed. She pulls the covers up and smooths them down over me. She says, "Hush," and pats me on the head. Then she goes out and comes back. She pulls the covers back down. She gets up on the bed. She puts her lips up against my ear. She whispers, "This will make him better." She says to me, "Hush, baby, sleep." She says, "Can't he go to sleep?"

She gets down again and gets between my legs. There is like this like noise of something—like these little noises of her doing something!

She goes, "There, is this better?"

Oh, Mr. Capote.

She says, "Is this too cold?" She says, "Is this too cold for baby?" She says, "Tell Mama if this makes him cold."

Oh, Mr. Capote, please!

She says, "Is it better now?" She goes, "Oh, isn't Noxzema just the thing for Mama's little baby?" She says, "Baby, baby, baby, does it sting where Mama fixed her little baby?" She says, "Tell Mama if it does."

Just the fingertips.

Just the fingernails.

Just the tippy-tips of everything!

I said, "I love you." I said, "Oh, my dearest, dearest."

She says, "Hush, baby, hush." She says, "Now you just go to sleep."

She pulls up a piece of the sheet. She gets it wrapped around my thing. She pats it down. She goes, "Oh, baby, he hurts all over." She says, "Oh, oh, baby."

She unwraps my thing. She says, "Shame on me, he's too hot. Oh, I made him so hot. See what I did? His little bandage is too tight. Oh, oh, let Mama fix it nice."

She gets it all off and she says, "How's this?" She says, "Oh, yes, Jergens is nice." She says, "Now, now, don't you dare let Mama hear you say Jergens is making him sting."

I said, "Oh, Janet Rose."

She says, "Is he cold?" She says, "Oh, I have to make him warm again." She says, "Oh, look what Mama did."

She puts it in her mouth. She puts it all of the way in. She goes this way and that way and this way and that way. She says, "Oh, he's so tired." She says, "Did Mama make him so tired he can't sleep?" She touches my thing with a finger. She says, "Oh, oh." She touches it with a fingernail. She says, "Can't baby go to sleep?" She goes around and around with her fingernail. Then she goes around and around again!

Oh, Mr. Capote, don't you see what I mean?

She says, "There, there, why can't baby sleep?"

She says, "I know what he needs."

She says, "Let Mama put more medicine on him."

She says, "Baby is so sick."

She says, "There, there."

She says, "Now hush, hush, now baby go to sleep."

She puts it in her hand and she gives it these like little tiny different squeezes.

She says, "Oh, oh, he is so cold again." She says, "Oh, how could he get so all so cold again?"

She puts it in her mouth. She moves her mouth all around. She says, "There, there."

She says, "Now hush-a-bye." She says, "Now go right to sleep right this minute." She says, "Shame on me, the doctor said give him his medicine." She says, "Oh, he needs more Noxzema." She says, "Now just you hush and be good." She says, "Mama says hush and be good."

Oh, Mr. Capote, don't you see what this is? It's the same thing as Ben Bernie! Only it's Janet Rose instead!

I can't help it. I get such a boner remembering. I just have to have these boners.

She makes rings with her fingers and puts the rings on.

She says, "There, there."

She says, "See what the doctor said for Mama to do?" She says, "Did you ever see a lassie go this way and that way and this way and that way?" Then this is what she does— goes this way and that way with her fingers like rings!

She says, "Hush, hush. Go to sleep."

Then she does what she just did again!

She says, "Did you ever see a lassie go this way and that way and this way and that way?"

I said, "Oh, my beloved, you are the most wonderful, wonderful human being."

She says, "Hush. Now you just hush now. Now you just make him be a good boy and just hush."

I said, "Oh, my beloved, my beloved, please!"

She says, "Please? Please? Can't the bad boy behave and just go right to sleep like Mama said?" She says, "Now baby roll over on his tummy and hush."

I said, "Oh, my beloved, please!"

She says, "There, there, just you hush and go to sleep."

I said, "Please, don't make me, please!"

She put it in her mouth. She put it in and took it out. She says, "There, there. Shh, shh."

She touched it with a fingernail. She says, "Now baby be a good baby and baby go to sleep." She touched it with a fingertip. She says, "Now let Mama see what is wrong with him." She made it bend the wrong way.

She said, "Oh, I know." She said, "I know why baby can't go to sleep." She said, "Baby can't go to sleep because he can't go to sleep." She says, "Do you want me to make him go to sleep?" She says, "If you want Mama to make him, you have to just say." She says, "Does baby want Mama to make him?" She says, "Just say and Mama will make him."

I said, "Oh, my dearest beloved, please!"

She says, "Oh, look!" She says, "Look what a full tummy he has." She says, "Does he have a tummy ache too? Is that why the bad boy can't sleep?" She says, "I know what." She says, "If he had an empty tummy, then he'd go right to sleep." She says, "Is this what baby wants Mama to do? You want Mama to empty his tummy?" She says, "Oh, the naughty, naughty little dickens, his little tummy just too full for him to go to sleep."

I said, "Oh, Janet Rose!"

She says, "But then Mama will have a full tummy instead of baby." She says, "Is that what baby wants?" She says, "Shame on him, the bad, bad boy."

She takes it with her hand and goes this way and that way and this way and that way.

"Oh," I said. "Oh."

"Oh," she said, "look what he did! Oh, the nasty, nasty dirty boy, look what he went and did, throwing up all over Mama! Shame on him! Shame on him! Shame, shame!"

She held it and squeezed it. She licked all of the you-know-what up from wherever it went. She came and put her lips on my lips. She squished it from her mouth into mine. It made a little sizzle sound. Then I squished it back into hers. This is what we did. We squished it back and forth. We just kept on squishing it until it was just spit and kisses—and then we fell to sleep.

OH, YOU SEE WHAT SHE WAS? She was the most wonderful thing anyone could ever think of! I mean, even if you think of T.C., could you ever think of Janet Rose?

You know something? Hey, this is really one for the books. I mean, you know what Janet Rose could do? She could do it just with talk! God is my witness, with just with talk! Now is this one for the books or is this one for the books? I'm serious. Janet Rose, all she had to do was talk and yours truly would get all of the way to his finish, end of discussion, period!

You take the last time I ever saw her. Meaning, when she says let's stand and look in the mirror. In other words, this is the mirror which was at Sylvia Berman's on somebody's closet named the Bermans. Hey, a person in your circle, I know I don't have to tell you this is a thing which well-off people have, mirrors on the doors of their closets, right? Be honest with me, how many houses do you have? So they all have mirrors on the doors of their closets or don't they, true or false?

Listen, I guarantee you, I wasn't born yesterday. I know what people have. Am I right or am I right?

So okay, so this is when yours truly last sees guess who, which is off-color, but you asked for it, so here goes. She says, "Look at us in the mirror together." This is what Janet R. says. She says, "Look at us naked in the mirror together. You are naked and I am naked and we are look- ing at each other in the mirror together. See my boobies? See my cunny? You can't see my hole when I'm standing this way, can you? You want me to show you my hole in the mirror? If I get down and I squat down and pull my knees out with my hands, then you could see my hole in the mirror. Do you want for me to do it? Maybe we would have to get up closer. Maybe you won't be able to see my hole from this far away. You want to go closer and I'll squat and pull out my knees out and you can take a good look? Then you can tell me what it looks like. Do you want to go closer to the mirror now? Or would you rather stay here and just look at my boobies and my cunny from where we are? Do you like my cunny better than my boobies? If I touched them, would you like my boobies better? Do you want to look in the mirror and see me touch my boobies? What do you like to call them? What is your favorite word? Look in the mirror and tell me what your favorite word is for everything you see. Or do you want me to turn around so you can see my other side? Do you want me to turn around and bend over and touch my toes? If I bent over like that, do you think you would see one hole or see both holes at once? Do you like my other hole as much as you like this one? Tell me if you are tired of looking at this hole and want to look at my other one now. Go ahead. You can tell me. Which hole? Do you want to look at the other one or at this one? I'll touch this one to show you what it looks like when I touch it. I'll put my finger in to show you. Which finger? You want me to use this one? Or this one? You tell me which one you want for me to use. Do you want to see me do it to myself? Look in the mirror and tell me if you do. It's different when you see it in the mirror, isn't it? Tell the truth, isn't it different when you see it in the mirror? Look, see me touch it with my finger? Is this the finger you for want me to touch it with? Do you want to lick it after I do it? What if I put it in my other hole? Would you lick it if I put it in the other one? Tell the truth. Would you? Would you really lick it? Look in the mirror. What if I went and got a hairbrush and put the handle in? What if I did it with a hairbrush? You think you'd like to see that? What if I went and got Syl and asked her to come in and do it to me with a hairbrush? Which would you like best, seeing me do it to myself or seeing Syl do it to me? Or what about seeing yourself? I know. What about another boy? Would you like to see another boy do it? Make believe there is somebody else and he is watching you watch me in the mirror. Go ahead and make believe that this is what is happening, that somebody is watching you watch me. What if it was Syl watching you watch? Make believe you are somebody else watching yourself.

Put your thing between your legs. Push it down and put it
in between them and hold them together like this. See?
You see? See how we look the same? But my hair is different. See how different it is? Look. Look in the mirror and
tell me how it's different. No, I know, tell me about Syl's.
What do you think Syl's is like? Do you want for me to
watch you touching Syl's? I'll go get Syl and then it can be
the three of us looking in the mirror together. Do you
want me to do that? Does it hurt like that when it is back
behind you like that? If I had one, I bet it would hurt me if
I did that. Does it hurt? Do you want for me to kiss it and
kiss it and make it stop hurting? If I kept on kissing it
enough, would it shoot off if I did? I know what. Make
believe I am doing it right now. Look in the mirror and
make believe I am doing it. Can you look in the mirror
and make believe? Make believe. Look at my lips. Look at
my lips in the mirror. See my lips in the mirror when I
talk? When I put your thing in, I go like this. Can you
look in the mirror and make believe you feel it? Look at
my cunny in the mirror and make believe you feel me
doing it. How does it feel? Can you feel me doing it? What
do you think it feels like for me when I feel your thing in
my mouth? Look in the mirror and tell me what you think
it feels like for me. Look in the mirror and tell me. If I
went and got Syl, would you tell Syl? Tell the truth, would
you like for me to go get Syl so you can? Would you like
for her to put your thing in her mouth? Would that be

something you would like? You can tell me. Look in the mirror and tell me. It's okay to say it if this is what you want. You want her to do it and for me to watch? She could get down here in front of the mirror and do it and you and I could watch. Is this what you would like? Would you like to see me watching you while you are watching Syl do it? Look in the mirror. Make believe. You see all of the things you can make believe if you have a mirror to help? You want for me to go get Syl? If we had Syl in here, think of all of the things we could do. Make believe she is. Make believe she is back behind you and she has got your thing and I am watching her do it to you. Look at me. Look at me looking at you look at me in the mirror. Watch my lips. See me doing it to myself with my finger? Am I using the finger you want me to? It's going to make you shoot off, isn't it? Go ahead. You can shoot off if you want to. Do it. Do you want me to hold it and do it? I would do it to make it shoot off for you, but I want to do it to myself. Shoot off. You have to shoot off because I said so. I think I am coming now and I want you to shoot off when I do. Oh, I am. Oh, I think I really am. Look in the mirror and look at my eyes in the mirror and you can tell from looking I really am. Look in the mirror. Look at my cunny in the mirror. Look at my eyes in the mirror. Look at me in the mirror! I'm coming, I'm coming, I'm coming, shoot off, shoot off! Oh God, I'm coming, shoot, shoot!"

It's the truth!

I did it just like she wanted me to.

Then she said she was only making believe.

Oh, Mr. Capote, don't you see?

Listen, I'll be honest with you, it just happened from me sitting here and saying what I just did.

Hey, I can tell you this, can't I? Did it lower me in your eyes? It didn't, did it? I mean, I have to let my hair down before we call it a day! Whoops, wait a minute. You think I'm going too fast? You think I need some breaths?

Let's face it, a certain individual really knew things. She knew everything. Janet R. knew these things which nobody ever even thought of! She always had a new one. She could talk you to your finish. Then she could give you another boner right after you just got through having one. Plus let's not forget something. She was thirteen! End of discussion, period.

Okay, correction. Okay, you caught me there on a little one, correction, correction! The thing is, she was fourteen the time I was just making mention of. Which was the last time when I saw her, plus time out for the interim when yours truly was you-know-where.

So do you blame me? I mean, one minute she was mine and the next minute was she?

Hey, I just remembered. *Interim.* This one was definitely one of them so far as far as Paki!

"Interim." I just remembered. "Interim." Except I don't have to tell you, yours truly only has to say it only once! Whereas you take the three questions or when they came in and said, "Drink it." Don't kid yourself. A certain some-body was no pushover! I promise you, they could have talked themselves blue in the face or stood on their left ear. But face facts, that's water under the bridge. You know what I say? I say you take the thing with the laces, that's water under the bridge! Forget it! Bygones is bygones. Hey, put it out of your mind. Plus definitely not in the book!

"Red Dog, Red Dog, this is Blue Dog calling, please come in!"

I miss him when he goes to sleep.

Here's something. You know what else?

I miss the people on the block before we moved. I miss the way they used to look at me. But I don't miss Davie or you-know-who. They changed. I don't miss someone who does. I just miss what they changed from and keep on wondering why they did it. But what's the percentage? Myself, I don't understand why everybody just can't be just like yours truly, which is like all of these different ways—you name them, you name them!—at once.

This is the thing about Ben Bernie!

You could always count on the Old Maestro. He was always there for everybody to count on, yours truly first and foremost! Will you just listen? *Au revoir, pleasant dree yums. God bless you and pleasant dree yums.*

SO THAT WAS WHERE I STAYED for a while when I first got to Gotham. Meaning, Janet Rose's mother's. She didn't care. She didn't pay any attention to me. She didn't pay any to Janet Rose either. She just got her bottle and sat there. Then she would take it and go off. If I was somewhere and she came in, she did not see me or even look.

As regards yours truly, I didn't go out. I just sat in the place and did whatever was quiet. I played the radio. It was dark in there. It was nice. It was always like five o'clock the season when the leaves fall off. Then when Janet Rose came home from the Bronx High School of you-know-what, she would go make the supper. It was just like she was the mother. She makes this, that, or the other thing, and we sit in the kitchen and eat it. Then you-know-who would come in and get more ice from the refrigerator and say, "Look at the little homemakers," or "Look at the little mister and missus." It's true, Mr. Capote. Yours truly and Janet R., we were Mr. and Mrs. First-Nighter, no kidding.

Sometimes I'd worry a little about a certain person. But not so much when you really come down to it. I'd say to myself, "Call her." But then I would also say to myself, "Let's not and say we did." Besides, I'll be honest with you. What if she asked me did I go in the water so Davie would have to come after me? Or what if she said she would kill me for making my brother get killed? Hey, you know what? I could have used one of Everett's icebreakers. But face it, who knew any of them back then?

Mostly what I did was sit around and get boners from

thinking about Janet R. coming home from you-know-where, that and what we were going to do when a certain someone's mother had enough you-know-what for herself and went somewhere to fall asleep.

Here's something! This is how yours truly got on the radio. In other words, just from being where he shouldn't have been or maybe it was vice versa. Hey, if present company had the time, I would keep getting it thought until I had it all thought through!

You'll see.

It starts with the time the mother got up and walked in when a certain individual was on the bed with his beloved on the bed and they were, you know, naked on it!

She didn't turn on the light. We didn't hear her open the door. She was just there in the room with us suddenly talking to us, sitting and talking to us in Janet Rose's chair. On the other hand, you probably couldn't say who she was talking to. Or even what she was saying. Maybe she just thought she was just talking. Or yours truly did. I don't know. But to my way of thinking, it was like a crazy person was there. Listen, I am not ashamed to say it. I was lying there thinking she is going to kill me because it made her crazy when she came in there and we were the way I said. Do you see what I am saying? You hear her saying these words, granted, but you can't tell. So in a manner of speaking, it's just like the Old Maestro all over again. Except it's vice versa!

We just laid there shaking like two leaves in a pod. But

maybe it was just me. Maybe it was only like one leaf. Listen, let's not kid ourselves. When it comes to Janet Rose, nothing ever made her scared. Long story short, Janet R. gives my hand a squeeze and goes ahead and gets up.

This is when I start hearing her say, "Mother?" But I don't hear the mother answering.

Janet Rose says, "Mother?"

But the mother goes on talking.

What's next is Janet Rose comes back to the bed and whispers for me to get up and go get in the living room and don't for me to try to do anything.

I did. I went back to the sofa and got under the blanket. I was really shaking. Then I see the light come on and I hear Janet Rose going like this. "Mother? Mother? Mother?" Listen, I won't kid you, it makes me too scared for me to be by myself. So far as I can see, it is just like the Plymouth all over again and somebody said, "I'll only be a minute." I mean, I held it and I held it, but I couldn't keep holding it anymore. So this is when I get the blanket around me and go to the door to look. Plus you know what? Mr. Capote, it is also the first time I see Janet Rose naked!

Oh, Mr. Capote, you should have seen! Little titties and everything! Oh, her privates with the hair on them! Take my word for it, I'm here to tell you, you will never know what you missed!

I say, "What's wrong? Is something wrong?"

But Janet R. just shakes her head. She says, "Mother?"

Then she comes into the living room and turns on the light by the telephone. She starts calling somebody and acting like there is a certain individual which is not even there.

I don't have to tell you, I can see everything now, all of the parts where she is white because she did not get a tan there. But I don't know if I got a boner from it or not. I mean, to my way of thinking, maybe I probably didn't because on account of being scared.

I say, "What's wrong? Is it my fault? Don't you think I better go get my things on and find a place to go?"

But she just waves her hand for me to be quiet and for me to leave her alone. Then she starts talking on the phone. It's her dad. I can tell it's her dad she's talking to. The other thing is, I can tell he doesn't care. You can always tell from somebody's face when somebody else doesn't care. So then she hangs up and calls somebody else. Granted, guess who was getting a little more scared. On the other hand, there's her titties, you know? Not to mention her backside and her you-know-what with the hair! But here's the best thing, which is her feet! Meaning, they are twice as good when you can see how they go with everything else Janet R. is letting you look at.

Hey, I almost forgot! The thing of it is, this is how I got to be friends with Janet Rose's mother's brother. It's also how I go from that stage of the game to being on the radio as a professional celebrity! In other words, Bill Lido.

Bill Lido took over.

PICTURE AN INDIVIDUAL with hair just like Janet Rose's. Except it goes without saying, he was as big as they come! In other words, this is the mental picture of Bill Lido. But just between you, me, and the lamppost, this was his name for strictly professional reasons. Meaning, like Scheindel Kalish and Ann Shepherd. Whereas I am just giving you my personal analysis. So don't quote me, okay?

Listen to this.

"This is the world's largest network, the Mutual Broadcasting System."

Here's another one.

"This is radio for all America, the Mutual Broadcasting System."

These are two of the station breaks which Bill Lido did. So enough said or enough said?

So the thing is, yours truly is there in his blanket when this individual comes over. This is interesting. Which is that no matter what the story is, Bill Lido is always smiling.

First thing he does is get out of his coat and start rubbing his big hands together. You can hear it, the noise he makes doing things. It's like a person who can come in the door and be inside and bring the outside inside with him.

God is my judge, I didn't notice how dark and quiet it was until Bill Lido came over and took over. This is the thing. You can see he is an individual which takes charge and doesn't wait for Peter and Paul! I'll be honest with you, yours truly felt better right away when Bill Lido was there.

You know something? I'd give anything to have Bill Lido here right now. Hey, could I give Bill Lido a list of things to take care of? I mean, how about starting with a ten-speed?

Okay, so the first thing the man does, Bill Lido gets the doctor for Janet R.'s mother, and after the doctor goes, he gets Janet R. and yours truly in the kitchen and says we have to have ourselves a chat for ourselves. He says, "Binny, how is school, how was Long Beach, you got a nice tan, just calm down, I'm going to get a practical nurse, everything is going to be all right." In other words, this is not a quote from Bill Lido himself, but I would have to say it is the nature of his conversation. The other thing is, he never stops smiling, even when he says, "Binny, who is this young man, what is he doing here, I am warning you, I am not your mother, be careful, young lady, don't you dare try anything cute with me, I will break every bone in your body." That wasn't a quote either, as it probably goes without saying. But it's me remembering.

Let's face it. What Janet R. couldn't handle they didn't invent yet, end of discussion, period!

She folds her hands and sits up straight and says it happens that a certain somebody is a nice boy and is an orphan and is running away from the Home of the Orphans of Long Island. She says I had my reasons, but they are too horrible for her to repeat. She says did he ever see Fascination? She says if he's seen it, then he knows where I was working, and this was because I needed the money.

You see what I mean? This is how a certain person could

handle a thing. Let's not kid ourselves. Was Janet Rose in a class by herself or was Janet Rose in a class by herself?

You want to hear something? Listen to this. When yours truly was you-know-where the second time, guess what they came and told me. They came and told me Janet Rose came to visit! They said she came all of the way up from Gotham by train. They said they couldn't let her see me on account of my condition! But you tell me, is that something or is that something? Because yours truly says it is!

Listen, feel free to use this in the book. What they said, that's a quote, I guarantee you. And I don't have to tell you, these are the people which everyone says are the experts. Don't worry, I'm serious. When it comes to the theories, these are the people which wrote the book!

But let's face it, Bill Lido wasn't born yesterday either.

So Bill Lido says, "The hell with it. I don't want to hear about it. I have got my hands full enough as it is."

To make a long story short, he throws all of the bottles out and goes to sleep on the sofa—whereas yours truly just stays where he was in the kitchen. The next thing is, Bill Lido wakes up smiling and makes Janet R. stay home from school. Me, he takes over to a hotel called the Ansonia. This is a hotel which is maybe three blocks from Janet Rose's. I won't lie to you. This was the first time guess who was ever really even outside in Gotham. So it stands to reason I would get a little sweaty, right? But Bill Lido says, "Don't worry, you'll be fine, a fine big boy like you."

It's true. It was like the times when I get sweaty and

sleepy both. You see what I am saying? It's a feeling like you are going slow and going fast and going more and more of it in both directions at once!

Listen, don't think I can't tell he wants to get rid of me. I personally am not pointing a finger at him for him wanting to do it. Bill Lido had his hands full, just the way I quoted. To tell you the truth, in my personal opinion, Bill Lido was as good as they come, like it or lump it. Even the time he held me against the building and got mad about the towel, I personally think he was doing the best anybody in his position could. Fair enough?

So getting back to the Ansonia, he gets me a room and pays for a week and gives me money. The other thing is, he says it is okay for me to talk to Janet R. on the telephone, but not ever to go back where she is. He says, "Son, I am taking care of everything, son. So you just look after yourself."

I don't have to tell you how I felt. I mean, it made me cry a little when he called me that. Also, this was my first time out of anybody's house. Don't forget, yours truly was fifteen and from somewhere else! So I just stay in the room all day the first day. I just stay in there and feel lonesome for Janet R. I didn't even go out to get anything for me to eat. What I did is I kept calling a certain person on the telephone and asking her if she could please come over. But she says she has to stay where she is because there is a nurse there and that if she didn't, the nurse would tell her uncle.

This is when I said why couldn't she talk to me the way she used to do it at night. But she said the nurse would catch her at it, whereas the thing for me to do was just to make believe she was doing it and spit in my hand and do it to myself, unless I had some Jergens.

So it goes without saying, I did it. I did it a lot of times the first day and more times the next. This is because the next day I went out and got some you-know-what. I got two bottles of it just to be on the safe side and keep having enough! But I guess I don't have to tell you it wasn't Noxzema, right?

Meanwhile, Bill Lido keeps on taking charge. For example, when the week is up, he gets me this other place, which was a room on West Eighty-fifth. It was really nice. It was in the apartment of this woman which had a son away at school and who was a widow. I say widow because this is what I think Bill Lido said. But maybe he didn't.

She said it was eight dollars a week, which was with breakfast every morning. She also said I didn't have to pay her for two weeks because Bill Lido already did. Well, talking about Peter to pay Paul, is that paying Peter to pay Paul?

It was very educational. She was a singer, I think. Or maybe she was just someone who wanted to be. I don't know. I never found out. In my analysis, it wasn't something you went ahead and asked. But the thing was listening when she practiced. In other words, scales and other things. The way it worked out at the start, I was always there to listen. Here's why. I didn't go out outside yet.

Number one, breakfast was plenty. Besides, she was always giving me more things for me besides. Number two, it was nicer inside. It was even nicer than Janet R.'s. There were books, just to begin with, books and things like that—you know, like pictures on the wall and so on. It was the first place I had ever seen which looked anything like that. You know what? To my way of thinking, it looked personally to me like the type of a place which Buddy Brown would live in if he grew up to have a place like that.

I was very neat about taking good care of my room. These things weren't my things. But yours truly made believe they were. I liked to tidy up. I spent a lot of time just making everything look tidied up and looking at the job I'd done. Also, I looked at the books in the room. Guess who the famous author of one of them was!

Hint: He wasn't a certain person who doesn't know better than to make his residence in the borough of Brooklyn!

I liked to touch the furniture, like the wood and all of that. There was a little statue of somebody. To my way of thinking, music had something to do with it—but this is just yours truly's educated guess. The thing is, I moved it from where it was to where the light from the window could stay on it longer. Another thing I did is look at it a lot and try to have slow thoughts for myself. Here's the one I tried the hardest to have. Her sitting in her chair sewing, me sitting on the hassock watching, the light coming in through the window the special way light can come in like that.

Guess who gives me some clothes her son used to use. She says they are too small, so feel free. Also, she tells me about the furniture and about the pictures and about everything I was always asking her about. It was so wonderful when she talked to me! Then she would stop and then start practicing again, and then yours truly would listen and sit there and make believe. You know what I would think to myself? I would think to myself, "Guess who is back before we moved back on the block back when he was still a picture-book boy and everything was different!"

Her name was Hirsch, Ruth Hirsch. Doesn't it sound like a woman like that? She was tall and had short brown hair. You want to hear something really crazy? She looked like my idea of how Barbara Luddy looked, even though I never saw Barbara Luddy! I mean, let's face it, Barbara Luddy's name! It makes you think of Janet Rose's hair and of Janet Rose's feet for you to hear Barbara Luddy's name, not to mention think of all of Ruth Hirsch!

I guess I don't have to tell you I was there only, you know, only a little while more or less. Plus, I suppose you know that now is when everything starts to go about seven zillion miles too fast! You don't understand yet—one minute listening to Ruth Hirsch sing, the next minute trying to listen to about seven zillion things. I don't know. In here is the hardest part for yours truly to tell you about. Maybe I should forget the whole deal. I am so tired already and, you know, this is just getting to the hardest part now!

I'll be honest with you. I don't know how much longer a certain person can keep sitting here and keep doing this. I mean, maybe this one is the wrong start too. Maybe I should have picked one of the other starts. Remember the first one—shake, rattle, and roll? So you tell me, you think I should have stuck to start No. 1? On the other hand, if I go back and start all over again, what about Norman? Believe me, this is what yours truly keeps asking himself.

Like, you know, what about Norman?

Hey, but let's not kid ourselves. I mean, if I went back, maybe I would get all of the way up here to here and it would be the same place for me all over again.

Listen, you know what I say? I say let's just get some deep breaths for ourselves and stop to think for a minute! Don't forget the time with Simon's, right? In other words, what if way back then I took the time to get some deep ones? Face facts, if a certain person took the time to breathe, he would be right there in the Plymouth and not in front of knives! On the other hand, don't forget what Everett says. Because doesn't everybody have to be some place or doesn't everybody have to be some place? Look at you, for instance! You could be in Gotham or the Hamptons or in Palm Springs or Palm Beach. Am I right or am I right?

Okay, deep breaths.

Deep breaths and sharpen Paki.

Deep breaths and get up and walk around the kitchen.

Hey, I'm just kidding. You can't really walk around this

kitchen! False alarm. Yours truly was just giving you an icebreaker for yourself. Maybe you can walk around yours, but mine—to tell you the truth, you could take my whole household and couldn't!

OKAY, SO TAKE IT OR LEAVE IT, here is what happens next. Bill Lido gets me into the show business!

It's like in the place there was this individual named Everett. But maybe I already made mention of him. So this Everett individual is always saying things, right? So one of the things he always says is this. "Sometimes I think it is better not to be born. But who is as lucky as that? Not one person in millions and millions of people!" So here is the point of me telling you this. It's like what Everett says goes for yours truly and the show business! I mean, it's like yours truly is the one person in millions and millions of people! What I am saying is, you have to give credit where credit is due. Unless you want to say it all goes to Janet R.'s mother on account of the time this person walked in. Well, who knows? You think I know?

Believe me, the answer is what's the diff when you really come right down to it. Because how can you give the credit to one individual in particular when if you really stop to think about it, you see where everybody plus Nature all pitched in? I mean, and don't forget Bobby R. too!

The thing of it is, Bill Lido gets his day off, and he comes over to Mrs. Hirsch's and he says for me to get ready, guess who is going to take me over to Mutual and show me how the radio works. So then he takes me over to Mutual and I meet these different people. Some of them do this and some of them do that. You know what? I was so excited, I couldn't even tell which was which or what!

So then he takes me downstairs for a malted, and he says, "How did you like it? Did you have a good time?"

I said, "It was the best time I ever had in all of my life forever." I said, "You won't believe this, but I thought the way it worked was different."

He says, "Really? Different how?"

I said, "I don't know. I just thought it worked different."

He said, "How did you think it did?"

I said, "I was little." I said, "Forget it." I said, "Do you know Ben Bernie or Barbara Luddy and Olan Soulé?"

He said, "First you tell me how you thought it worked."

I said, "How come you call her Binny—you and Mrs. Rose?" I said, "Is there a reason for that, Binny?"

He said, "All you have to do is stay away from her. Do we have an understanding? I've done some things for you. Now you do one or two things for me."

I said, "Oh, sure. She's only thirteen."

He said, "I'm glad you're cooperating. You just keep on cooperating with me, and I will do my best to work with you. Do we have a deal?"

I said, "I am doing my best to cooperate."

He said, "Good. Now how would you like it if I got you a job around here? Do you think you'd like a thing like that?"

So there was the whole thing of it right there! I mean, just like that, Bill Lido popped the question! All yours truly had to do was sit and nod his head. On the other hand, let's not kid ourselves, there was more to it than I am in a position to actually go ahead and tell you. In other words, you don't get to be a famous celebrity on the radio without somebody pulling the strings for you! I'll just put it this way. Let's just say if you know the right people, you know the right people! Meanwhile, long story short, one thing leads to another. The rest is inconsequential. Yours truly could talk himself blue in the face, and present company still would not get all of the ins and outs of it! Let's face it, it's like present company trying to tell me how he got to be a famous celebrity himself! You had to be there, right? Your layman doesn't understand this! But speaking as one professional celebrity to another, the less said the better! I mean, it would be way over the people in the public's head to begin with. In all modesty, when it comes to the complicated parts, the book can get along without it! So this is why yours truly will just skip to what you've been waiting to hear about. Which is that the first program a certain somebody was on was called *My True Story*. Naturally, the star of this was Bobby Readick, not to mention Ann Shepherd!

True or false, Ann Shepherd was really Scheindel Kalish?

So the thing of it is, yours truly's voice goes out to all of the radios all over everywhere. Which means also to the ones in, you know, in Long Beach!

But let's not kid ourselves, this was just for openers. The next thing I know, yours truly doesn't know whether he's coming or going. Believe me, that's how fast Nature was taking its course. *Big Sister, Stella Dallas, Bulldog Drummond, Dr. Christian, Boston Blackie, The Romance of Helen Trent, Portia Faces Life, Our Gal Sunday, Hilltop House, When a Girl Marries, Lorenzo Jones, The Guiding Light, Hop Harrigan, Mr. District Attorney, Counterspy, Captain Midnight, One Man's Family, Jack Armstrong, Grand Central Station, Inner Sanctum, Suspense,* I was on all of these different programs. And that's not the half of it! But I am not here to tell you how famous a celebrity I was. In all humility, I was. Whereas the all-important one to make mention of is *Young Doctor Malone*—starring, you guessed it, Bobby Readick until he vomited, but yours truly when he did!

Wait a minute! Did I make reference to the fact that Ann Shepherd was my co-star when I starred on it? Except to me she was really, you know, Scheindel Kalish!

It goes without saying, I was making good money. Granted, we don't have time for us to get into a discussion of the dollars and cents of the situation. Let's just put it this way. I was making enough of it to take some of it and send it to a certain someone back in the town of Long Beach! What I did was I wrote a letter which said, "Here is some money. I am fine. Everything is fine. Turn on the radio and I will say hello." Then I folded the whole thing inside some brown paper before I put it in the envelope and sent it. Which is the other rule my dad taught me to do back when you-know-who also taught me for me to always make sure you have a dollar in your pocket. In other words, you don't want the people in the public which have the job of delivering the letter for you for them to know there is money in there in the letter!

"Red Dog, Red Dog, do you read me, do you read me?"

I kept some left over for me for this, that, and the other thing. Don't think I didn't know about getting ready for your rainy day. This is why I put it under the box which Mrs. Hirsch had on the floor in the back of my closet. You know what I always say? I always say better safe than sorry! Enough said? Here's something. I mean, it goes without saying, putting it in the box is what your average individual would say to himself for him to do. Whereas you know what your smart money does? Your smart money puts it under the box. Besides, my Jergens was in the box, okay?

I remember when I did it. This is because I remember all of the time I took making up my mind about in or under, and about how I kept looking at the little statue when I did it. The other thing is, this is the same day when you-know-who and a certain person get back together again, but only in a manner of speaking. How it worked was this. I waited until Mrs. Hirsch went out to get the shopping done. Then I got the Jergens and called Janet Rose.

First I give her all of the news, and tell her all of the various different programs for her to listen for me on! Then she says she is making a zillion notes and she will if she is not in school when they are all on. So then it is my turn to tell her how I can disguise my voice this way and that way and so on and so forth. Then she says she can't listen so much in the first place on account of school and homework. So next thing is I tell her that's okay, that she is my beloved anyway, and how the day will come when we will be together again as Mr. and Mrs. First-Nighter again! Whereas that in the meanwhile I cannot go back on her uncle, seeing as how I gave him my word to him as a gentleman and that everything I am today I owe to him, end of discussion, period.

She says, "Okay, now put some Noxzema in your hand and do everything exactly how I tell you."

I go, "I don't have any. Can't I use Jergens?"

She goes, "Do you love me or do you love me?"

I go, "I was only just kidding. It was right here all of the time. I've got a nice fresh jar of Noxzema."

I'll be honest with you. I didn't really have it. Let's face it, I thought about going out to get some, but then I had this other thought, which is Mrs. Hirsch is coming back!

She says, "Okay, now get your thing out and get ready."

Oh, Mr. Capote, I am getting myself a boner again!

She says, "The nurse might come. You have to hurry." She says, "Do you want me to do it to myself while you are? You can tell me if you do. But I can't. I can't because I don't want to. But you can do it for the both of us. Will you do it for both of us? So did you get it yet? Did you go get it before I told you to? He's sticking up, isn't he? Tell the truth, he is, isn't he? Look at it and tell me how it looks—does it look all red and veiny? Put the Noxzema on. See how white it makes it look? Put it all over. That's right, that's right. Oh, God, I can feel you doing it. Can you feel me feeling you do it? I have to whisper softer. Hold the phone tight to your ear so I can whisper softer. Oh, oh, it feels so good. Do you hear me? What should I say next? You have to tell me what to say next. You tell me and I'll say it. It's all right—you can tell me to say anything you want me to and I'll say it. Or maybe you want Mrs. Hirsch to. Or my mother. Did you ever notice my mother? Oh, I've gone and wrecked it, talking about my mother. Did I make it go all saggy? He was all stiff and trying to be big and look what Mama did. I made him get all tiny again, didn't I? Tell me the truth, didn't I? Oh well, have to fly, Latin and geometry, Peter and Paul. Good-bye, my Abelard, good-bye."

Did you hear that?

What was that?

Oh, Mr. Capote, I'm so tired!

I have to be honest with you. I am too worn out for me to sit here and be cute with you anymore! I mean, at this stage of the game, what's the percentage in playing footsie with you? Norman, he definitely held it against me because with him I kept letting my hair down with him too much.

So here is the thing. Speaking to you as one professional to another, here is the thing. Do you think you-know-who really was nuts about me, or do you think a certain individual was just making believe?

Stop and think a minute, and then tell me what you think. It's just that this is the question, so don't make me repeat it! I mean, if she really was, then how come she goes right that minute out and buys Scotch tape for the refrigerator when she could have just waited for when she could go ahead and pick some up the next chance she gets on the job at her, you know, at her McCrory's or wherever? Because I ask you. In all honesty, yours truly wants to ask you this question. Was it to stick his picture on the refrigerator right that minute or his? Whereas didn't she say it was always yours truly which was always the picture-book boy?

LISTEN, LET'S STOP KIDDING OURSELVES! No offense, but I don't exactly have all night, okay? You see what I'm saying? So you tell me, when do we get to wheel and deal? Believe me, I am not pointing any finger. But who's kidding who? I mean, with Norman you could talk turkey right off the bat with him as regards your terms and your general what-have-you. On the other hand, I can see how with present company it's not strictly a question of business is business. In other words, you are an individual with feelings. I promise you, this is something I take my hat off to you for, letting me let my hair down with you and not making me stand on ceremony with you! But let's be honest with each other, some things we definitely don't need in the book on a bet!

For instance, there is the call I make after the one I just told you about, which because it is a long-distance one, yours truly goes out to do. Okay, here is the mental picture. Number one, I put the Jergens back in the box and get out the money from under it. Number two, I walk over to the corner and go into a telephone booth. So are you following me so far or are you following me so far?

I say, "It's me. Guess what. I was Young Doctor Malone on your favorite program. Bobby Readick had to vomit, so I was. I love you and I miss you and I am sorry to God for everything. Did you hear me? If you were listening, you did. I was Young Doctor Malone."

She says, "That's nice. I am the Queen of England." She says, "So this is where you have been—in the crazyhouse?"

I said, "I am on the radio. Sometimes the celebrities get sick. He was vomiting. You said it was your favorite. You know who Bobby Readick is? He had to vomit. He tried and tried but could not catch his breath."

She says, "He's not the only one who has to vomit." She says, "Where are you?" She says, "I want the truth."

I said, "It's okay. Everything is all right. I am on the radio." I said, "I am on everything." I said, "Didn't you used to say it was the one you liked the best?"

She says, "I have had it up to here with you." "I want the truth," she says. She says, "Do you realize you are as out of your mind as you-know-who?"

I said, "Write down what I am going to be on. You can listen to me whenever you want." I said, "I miss you. I love you. What do you think about me being Young Doctor Malone?" I said, "Did you get a pencil?" I said, "Because I am sorry Davie died. Do you have the pencil?"

She says, "What died! He's saying what died? What is the lunatic talking about?"

I said, "I didn't do anything." I said, "God punished him for Buddy Brown."

She says, "What him! Buddy Brown? Listen to me, do you know what the meaning of the word lunatic is? For your information, do you?"

I said, "You know what Davie did?"

She says, "As God is my judge, when he was a baby, I knew." She says, "Is this the punishment I get for you-know-when?" She says, "Two adults, but the child is still trying to kill me for it." She says, "Is this what a mother gets from a child, death?"

I said, "I was making it all up. I never heard anything in any vacuum. You're crazy for thinking I did."

She says, "I cannot believe my ears. I hear him, but I cannot believe it. Nobody could, not even a saint."

I said, "Please, oh God, please."

She says, "Are you finished? So are you finished with

your pleases?" She says, "So what is it you want from me? You want to hear a scream from me?" She says, "Is this it? You have to hear your mother scream? Because here is what you can do with your pleases." She says, "Do not call me. Do me a favor and do not call me with your pleases and with your Davies, not to mention with your Buddy Browns. Call him. Tell him."

I said, "Him?"

Then she hangs up. Then I call her back. But I just listen to her listening to me wait. You think she wanted for me to wait for only a minute? Icebreaker, icebreaker, ha ha.

She says, "You want his number? You didn't know I had his number? Listen, dummy, you think I did not have it from the word go? So for your information, the man is in Atlantic City. So you tell me, Mister Young Doctor Malone, you have heard of Atlantic City? Because this is where the son of a bitch is dancing in the streets. So you want the number? So here is the number."

I'LL BE HONEST WITH YOU. I just stood there in the booth trying to think some slow thoughts. Then I went and got more change and told the operator the number to call. But it just rings and rings. So then I call Janet R.'s. But it's busy. This is when I get the operator again. But it's no use. It's just like always—somebody always saying sit tight, they will only be a minute.

Listen, I won't kid you. I don't remember the bus ride. To

tell you the truth, the same thing goes for getting from the phone booth to where the buses leave from. But to my way of thinking, it is not such a big deal if you don't. Face it, does yours truly remember all of the Ben Bernie thing when the Old Maestro signed off the air yet? Okay, so what I remember next is calling from the depot in Atlantic City and this woman which answers and goes, "I don't care who you are, you got a lot of nerve calling people at an hour like this."

I said, "Is my father there, please?"

She goes, "Who's this?"

I said, "Is my father there, please?"

She goes, "You sure you got the right number?"

I said, "It's the one they gave me. It's the right number. May I please speak to my father there, please?"

She goes, "Honey, the poor guy is out like a light, honest. You think you could call back in the morning? Where you calling from, honey? I'll have him call you right back in the morning, all right?"

I said, "I can't stay here. I'm where the buses come in. Can you give me the address?"

She says, "You have your sisters with you, hon?"

I said, "I don't know anything about any sisters." I said, "Just tell me what the address is."

She says, "You promise you won't ring the buzzer until eight?" She says, "Just don't ring it until it's eight."

Oh, Mr. Capote, I couldn't really see much until it started to get light. But when it did, I could see it wasn't a house or anything like that. Let's just say it was more like, you know, like a so-called motor court, except the cabins had long numbers instead of short ones. Also there was this tiny little window to one side of the door. In other words, no kidding, it is like this little house in a picture book! But the thing of it is, they wouldn't really put one like it in it.

YOU WILL NOT BELIEVE THIS, but I was not sitting there thinking what you think. I mean, it sounds crazy for yours truly to say it, but a certain someone was just thinking just about the curb. Also, how he was inside probably looking out the little tiny window at me watching me sit on it across the street. But you know how thoughts are. Let's face it, when all is said and done, what are your thoughts except just one of those things? You take right now, for instance, what my thoughts are. You see what I'm saying? I mean, I just had a zillion billion more of them the minute I just stopped for me to tell you. Hey, forget it. Like just for openers, get this—the Maybelline and the hairbrush and the click. On the other hand, it makes sense to think about a curb. In other words, I was thinking about him looking out the window and seeing somebody who was thinking about what he was sitting on. Here is the thing—I wanted a certain somebody to see I was being a boy waiting!

The other thing is, it was cold. What makes it even colder is this pink bird which is up on one leg in front of the place. I don't know. It was like one of the things they give you at Fascination if you get a good enough score and you win. So yours truly keeps thinking to myself did you-know-who win one of those? You know what? I even thought he maybe made a deal where he wasn't supposed to ever let anybody ever know, which was probably why he had to go away. Well, I just thought I would tell you one of the thoughts I was having while guess who was sitting waiting for it to be eight o'clock.

But let's be honest with each other, I don't think I waited long enough. I mean, number one, a watch is something I more or less didn't have on me at the time. So what I did was I just said to myself, "Okay, it is eight o'clock." This was when I got up and went across and pushed the button under the number and waited for my father to come. You know what? I think it was probably a number like the number which is on the blade of Paki. But I can't say one way or the other if it was, so don't quote me, promise?

The door opens just like that.

But it's not my dad. It's this woman with frizzy hair. She has on a bathrobe on and frizzy slippers. She just looked frizzy to me as a person all over.

She says, "Harry, your kid's here!"

I am just standing there. I am thinking about the name she said and about when I heard them in the closet. I am thinking about how you open the door and there you are in Simon's! Then there is this man there where I can see him and he can see me. Hey, it makes me stop and think when I stop to think about this.

He says, "That's not my kid."

She says, "How come he's not?"

He says, "Get rid of him."

She says, "You get out of here now. You got the wrong people. Go look for some other people."

Mr. Capote, I'm telling you, she shuts the door on me! Mr. Capote, yours truly is telling you, yours truly is just standing there as a human being!

Then it opens up again. He says, "Beat it!" But God is my judge, I couldn't! You want to hear the whole thing of it? Mr. Capote, I couldn't!

So you tell me, you think yours truly was just making believe he couldn't? I don't know. Maybe it was a certain person just wanting the door to see a boy which couldn't. You think this was what it maybe was? Listen, if this is your personal opinion, I would be the first one to tell you maybe yes and maybe no.

Meanwhile she's tapping on the little tiny window waving for me to get away. Then he opens up the window and says, "Come on, you heard me, punk, scram!" But yours truly was just somebody standing thinking how guess who was somebody who can't move.

The police come! An ambulance comes! There is all this noise! There is the door opening, the door closing, people moving, people talking, the little tiny window going up and going down and me going up going down onto this thing which rolls and rolls. Then there is this man which has what you feel is a wind with him just like Bill Lido did with him. Mr. Capote, how come is it there are some people and others? This is a real question.

He says, "We'll just get this tight here."

Then somebody else says, "Okay, fellas, upsy-daisy."

CAN YOU BEAT IT? I MEAN, God is my judge! Because it just dawns on me about at lunchtime today. I mean, the fatty with the bike! Remember the one which was walking it and this thing in the back of her eye just keeps coming out? So it just comes to me, it was on the way to Peartree's, right? In other words, this is the direction she was going in, true or false? Whereas does yours truly have to tell you it is also the direction of where a certain famous celebrity happens to have his residence when he is at home at his residence in Gotham? You see what I am saying? I mean, is this one for the books or is this one for the books? Talk about your small world! Talk about one thing always leading to another! This one is really one for the books! I mean, the envelope in her basket! Granted, I didn't stick around to check it out. But it was this big official-looking envelope! I mean, talk about your nutty coincidences! But didn't I tell you everything leads to another thing? So what was it, something for you to sign or something like that? Because I promise you, it is a top-ten bank! Hey, you know as well as I do, whatever it was, my branch will get right on it, don't kid yourself. Let's face it, I am probably wasting my breath. They probably already sent it over via somebody else! You know what? I would not be one bit surprised if you told me one of the officers went ahead and handled it themselves! On the other hand, there's no telling. Put it this way. One of the authorities maybe said to themselves, "This is evidence." But here is the thing. So what if it is? Because is it fair to take it out on a certain famous celebrity?

Listen, let's just for argument's sake say this. It is a question of time, and guess who does not have to tell a certain person time is money! Fair enough. So this is why yours truly says forget it, he will make it up to you in so many dollars and cents. In other words, you figure up what it comes to you in so many dollars and cents, and we will go ahead and take that figure at face value and deduct it from the boy's end—no arguments, no discussions, no explanations, period! Believe me, I wouldn't even say to you how you should maybe get down on your hands and knees and thank me for keeping a fatty like that away from your line of vision. I mean, let's not kid ourselves. What came out after Paki came out, it could have been from something which is catching! I am just saying better safe than sorry.

So are we talking about letting bygones be bygones? I promise you, as far as yours truly is concerned, it is all ancient history at this stage of the game. You watch.

Believe me, it will make your head spin to see how fast I meet a person halfway and make amends! So be honest with me. Am I back in your good graces or am I back in your good graces? Because, number one, can I wave a wand? Whereas, number two, I don't have to tell you what time it is and what the conversation was when this thing came up and it got us off the proverbial track. Enough said?

So long story short, the next thing you know, they take me out and roll me in somewhere. Then this individual comes over to me and asks me what my name is. Okay, so this is crazy. So you know what I said? I said, "Young Doctor Malone is." So then this other individual comes over to me and he looks down at me and he gives me this look, you know? Whereupon he says to me am I or am I not ready to say who I am?

Look, yours truly promised you aboveboard, and aboveboard, believe me, you will get!

I think a certain someone was making believe!

Face it, yours truly can't tell you the name of the place they took me to next. I just know it was somewhere in Jersey and up high on a hill. The second thing is, the people in the public there kept saying hello to me when I got there. Everybody was very polite. You know what? Guess who thought it was just a check to see if I had good manners. I thought if they thought I had them, they would let me go. Or maybe it was the opposite. I don't know.

I said, "Hello." I said, "Good morning."

Then this fellow came over and undid the straps.

He said, "How do you feel?"

I said, "Fine, thank you."

He said, "Good, good." He said, "That's very good." He said, "Now on your feet, you little prick."

HEY, I JUST THOUGHT OF SOMETHING.

T.C.'s Devil's heel. You think Paki could reach it better than my you-know-what could? Not that you should ever stick a knife in a place like that! You take Janet R. sticking the hairbrush handle there. Was there ever anything crazier or was there ever anything crazier?

I'll be honest with you. The worst face I ever saw is when you-know-who got it up there and she says to me she is going to keep it up there until she gets to her finish. But the thing of it is, it was just another fake face.

Hey, I made plenty myself! I mean, when yours truly was sitting waiting on the curb. I kept trying out these different faces for me to get ready for the right one for my dad. Hey, you know what? I used to love to sit like that, on a curb just being quiet. Tell the truth. You did too! Am I right or am I right? In my analysis, you look like an individual like that when I see you in Peartree's! Answer me this. Is it the same way with you like it is the way with me? Because with me, it makes me feel funny-feeling just to sit and look. You know what I am saying? It gives me a funny feeling just looking but on purpose not seeing!

I miss him so much. I never missed anything the way I miss him so much. I miss him right this minute. Listen, a certain somebody is going to be forty-eight next birthday, but all he does is miss him so much. Face facts, it's him and Ben Bernie! Not to mention you-know-who when he has to go to sleep or school.

"Red Dog! Red Dog! This is Blue Dog—answer, please!"

Oh, hey, look who you-know-who forgot! Peter plus Paul (joke), plus Janet R., ha ha.

So this was the first place. I was in it for sixty days. They said yours truly was in it on account of C.O., which is Constant Observation.

"Red Dog, Red Dog, please come in!"

The cell they had for me, it's under the roof and there is a leak in the roof because of, you know, its probably the rain. The other thing is, they come in and belt me to it with belts. Meaning, this kind of funny-looking bed they had. Then they come in and use manacles instead. Let's face it, it's just like in the comic books! Except yours truly has to do my business right there in the bed-looking thing. Hey, you tell me—is this anything they would show you in a comic book? Meaning, the number two has to go under me! But as regards the number one, it runs all over and burns. Then the next thing is, they only come in sometimes. They come in and feed me with a big spoon and give me some water sometimes. Hey, it's oatmeal!—I think it's oatmeal, no kidding! Big deal! Am I a good sleeper or a good eater? They come in at night. They put a blanket on me at night. They say for me not to cry at night.

So that's it and that's it. In other words, it's how many days? It's sixty days! So then they give me back my stuff! They take me downstairs and hand me over my money and tell me for me to call someone to for them to come get me. So I look at the Yellow Pages and call a taxi. Some of them say it's too far. Then there is one which says he's on the way! Listen, what choice does yours truly have but for him to be honest with you? So listen—when the driver asks me where to, a certain somebody gives the same address!

THIS TIME THERE IS A CHRISTMAS WREATH on the little tiny window, not to mention also one on the bird. The other thing different is it is him which opens the door and a different-looking woman. This one you can see everything! God is my witness, you could! You know how they have this like this wet-looking hair which looks like it's sticking out around their underpants just the way I once saw with, like with Janet R?

He says, "What's the matter with you?"

I said, "Do you know where my father is, please?"

He says, "Kid, I'm asking you nice—you want me to split your head wide open for you?"

She says, "For Christ's sake, Harry, get back in here!"

He says, "Get back in there yourself! Can't you see the nut is looking at your twat!"

I said, "Tell him just for him to keep checking out the Mutual Broadcasting System. Plus tell him Davie's dead."

She says, "You feel sick, sonny? You want to wait right there while I get somebody to help?"

He says, "Yeah, you wait right there." Then he gets her by her hair and shuts and locks the door.

Here's something. All of the way back to the bus station, I keep telling the driver how I can't get over it, the fact that it is Christmas and I did not get anybody any presents yet and so guess who is going to have to rob Peter to pay Paul for them. But don't kid yourself. I was just fooling around. It was just to get some practice as far as talking again.

Whereas take you, on the other hand, you could talk the arm off the proverbial Chinaman. Am I right or am I right? Hey, who's kidding who? Yours truly has sat here and seen present company on Johnny's, and I say more power to you! Listen, if I could talk like you and Norman, you think I would not go on all of the channels and do it? But forget it, okay? One thing a certain person would never do is try to horn in on things when you and Norman are talking to Johnny on that particular channel.

Okay, so you caught me again! Face facts, they sign off on 13 what? Ten, eleven, something like that? Meanwhile yours truly is no sleeper, so where do I go from here? So I watch a certain channel a little bit, is this such a crime? On the other hand, you take T.C. and what her theory is. Which is that if it is not *Charlie's Angels*, you might as well go get some shut-eye and that's that!

Hey, time out. I was just wondering something. I mean, for argument's sake, when you go on as a famous celebrity on Johnny's with Norman! I mean, like beforehand or like afterwards, I was just wondering if you two fellows ever sit down together and break bread together, things being what they are. I mean, it just dawns on me to ask. But let's not be ridick, okay? You and Norman breaking bread together what with the way things are? Hey, I really had to be some kind of a nut or something for me to come up with a crazy one like that!

So level with me, after Johnny's or beforehand, when you fellows have to go to a place to party, do you give the nod to the C.B. or do you give the nod to the C.B.? Not that you have to tell me if it's something you have to keep private. Believe me, I have plenty of my own private things for me to keep private too! Let's just put it this way. If yours truly started telling you all of his, you and yours would go through the proverbial roof!

I DID NOT DO A LOT OF TALKING going back on the bus. But it was more on account of being lonely-feeling than of on account of not practicing anymore. But when I get to Mrs. Hirsch's, forget it as far as everything! This is because it is not Mrs. Hirsch but somebody who says Mrs. Hirsch moved away. So I tell them I have to get my things. But they say there aren't any for me to get. So I tell them I have to get my statue. But they say no dice, no nothing, they cannot permit entry for me to run a check. So I tell them they should tell me where Mrs. Hirsch moved to so I can see her and ask her about this and that. But they say they are not at liberty to offer this information to every Tom, Dick, and Harry which comes around. This made me stop and think. You know, the name Harry? So then I take a deep breath and tell them they should call Mrs. Hirsch and ask her if she can do it. But they say they do not have the authority to call a long-distance call.

I say, "Give me the number so I can."

They say, "Not without permission of the party in question." They say, "Show us written permission."

I don't know. I just could not think of any more things for me to say after that. But maybe it was because you get out of practice when you have been, you know, away in a place.

Granted, I didn't want to go against Bill Lido. But look at it this way. Where was the choice? So guess who goes you-know-where! Because that's where I went.

Can you believe it? It is the mother herself who buzzes back the buzzer when yours truly buzzes it downstairs. I said, "It's me." I was too cold for me to stop and think of anything else for me to say. I go, "I know I'm not supposed to be here, but it's me and I have to be."

The buzzer buzzes and I go in and then go up. She's got the door open when I get up. In other words, a certain individual is holding the door open like she can't wait for me to get inside. But you think I can't see she is changing her mind as soon as she sees me?

She says, "You sounded like somebody else."

You know what? Guess who is not wearing anything but a robe! You want to hear something else? Here is something else. Yours truly could smell it! Meaning, your alcoholic type of beverage!

She says, "Look, if you want Binny, she's not here. She went out with some friends to the movies." She says, "You know my brother was looking for you? Didn't he get you a job as a messenger somewhere? I thought he got you some kind of a job like that over at Mutual as a messenger over there. So you just walked out on it, is that nice? After Billy knocked himself out for you, is that nice? Don't you have a coat or something?" She says, "Wait a minute, did you ever lay a finger on my kid? Answer me, how far did you go with her? Do you want to tell me or would you like to explain it to her father?" She says, "Didn't Billy warn you not to come around here again? If you want to do it to somebody so bad, go pick on somebody else." She says, "You little dope, don't you know what you could get for messing around with a girl under-age? You want to spend the rest of your life behind bars? If Billy knew you were here, he'd tear you limb from limb. Is that what you want? Do you want it so bad you wouldn't care if you got yourself torn apart for it? You must want it awful bad to get yourself torn apart for it." She says, "Is that how bad you want it?" She says, "You're a lulu, you know that? You must be some kind of a fruitcake to come around here after what my brother said to you. What's the

matter with you, you all hot and bothered and there's no little chippie for you to play house with?" She says, "You hear
me?" She says, "The cat got your tongue?" She says, "What
are you, all little birdie and no mouth?" She says, "Boy,
could I teach you a thing or three, all little birdie and no
mouth." She says, "What's the matter, sweetie, the gals
making it hard for you?" She says, "Is this what it is, too
hard for you?"

Mr. Capote, wild horses could not make you believe
what a certain individual reaches out her hand and does
with it next, plus with her other hand makes her robe
come open so you can see it for a minute open!

She says, "Let's just see what he's got there." She says,
"You call this something?" She says, "I call it nothing."
She says, "Binny got herself all excited over a little baby
birdie like this?" She says, "Jesus, you're some fruitcake,
you know?" She says, "That Binny, my God!"

She takes her hand away and goes back inside the door.
She says, "Come take a bath." She says, "You want to come
in and take a bath?" She says, "I was just going to go take a
bath." She says, "Come on, you come take a bath."

I said, "If I could just get warm."

She says, "A bath will get you good and warm." She
says, "A bath will get you nice and warm." She says, "There
is nothing like a nice bath for it to make a person feel nice
and warm."

It was something, seeing the room again, seeing the

sofa again, seeing the whole place again! I just stood there giving everything a good look.

She says, "Come on, we'll get nice and warm."

Mr. Capote, the next thing is, I'm telling you, a certain somebody and her are you-know-where!

She says, "You'll feel nice and warm once you get inside a nice warm tub."

The steam was the main thing. So does present company see what I am saying when I say it was the steam? And the smells! Like perfumes smells and things! Oh, Mr. Capote, it was so nice and warm which was the main thing!

She says, "Oh, look what's here."

It was a bottle on the back of the toilet. She took it and sat down on the toilet. She says, "Now this is what I call cozy." She puts her head back and gets the bottle set for her to drink from it. Yours truly could see the things in her neck! It is like these little things which are under the skin when they drink! She says, "This is really cozy and warm." She pushes the door shut with her foot. She says, "Go have a bath." She says, "I've seen people take a bath before." She says, "Let's see that little birdie of yours." She reaches her hand over and puts her fingers in the water. She says, "Come on, sweetness, we don't have all night."

You think yours truly can tell you how he gets on the floor? My theory is it is on account of the steam. I don't know. I think the steam made a certain person feel he had to feel sleepy-feeling and fall asleep.

Here's something. The fuzz of the bath mat! There was a bath mat! There was fuzz in my mouth or frizz in my mouth! Then there was her foot! Does present company believe this? Mr. Capote, Mrs. Rose has her foot on my head!

She says, "Look." She jiggles her foot and says, "Look." She says, "It's okay, you can look." She says, "Everybody likes to look."

Oh, Mr. Capote, guess who has her robe all opened up and also are her legs!

She says, "It's okay, I swear." She says, "Here, you touch it here." She says, "You see where I am right here?" She says, "Come kiss me right here where my finger is here."

You know something? Can I tell you something? Because T.C.'s definitely got something when the woman says it's, you know, it is like a little heel where the Devil jumped in and left his heel sticking out. But I don't know. There are some others of them which don't!

So as far as present company, when personally do you think a certain individual started screaming? I mean, you think it was before or after when Janet R. walks in? But then look out—because they both of them were screaming at once. It was worse when yours truly started too. But here is the thing of it. They stopped. Janet R. and Mrs. Rose stop. But guess who couldn't? So can you guess who couldn't?

So you think this is why she cracked me with the bottle? In other words, you think it is? On the other hand, I will be honest with you. Who knows which one did!

I said, "I am going to fall down."

Someone said, "He's crazy, can't you see?"

I said, "I have to stop and get my breath."

I think I got down on the floor. But a certain person could not catch his breath! So this must be when they went and turned everything on. They turned on the faucets! They turned on the radio! They turned on the vacuum! Yours truly could hear all of the motors running calling *Davie*.

BILL LIDO HAD ME when I woke up. I don't mean he waked me. I just mean he had me with him when I did. I mean he was holding me up.

I could tell it was not in the bathroom anymore. But I did not know we were outside until I felt how cold it was. But then I felt it and felt how he had me up against the building. So then I knew I was outside and that there was something which was wrong.

You know what? In my personal opinion, there was snow coming down. But maybe it wasn't. Here's something. There was this towel on my head! Bill Lido put my hand up there for me to feel it. He kept putting my hand up there and telling me for me to hold it there so it wouldn't fall off from there. The other thing is, I can't. This is because the sleeve of the coat they went and put on me is too tight for me to get my arm up that high enough.

It's crazy, but I smell Jergens. No kidding, it is what Bill Lido's mouth smelled like to yours truly, like Jergens is in his mouth. You know what I thought? I thought to myself maybe the people on the radio have to do this because of some reason. So what do you think? Does present company think they all have to put Jergens in their mouth for some reason? Or is this theory just too crazy for words?

I said, "How come people call her Binny?"

He says, "Keep your hand up here like this."

Be honest with me, you do or you do not think people have to put Jergens in their mouth for some reason? So what about on TV and Johnny? I know it sounds like this is probably a crackpot theory, but there is no telling if you are in the know or not in it, is there? Listen, it couldn't hurt to ask around. I mean, don't forget what a certain someone always says. Live and learn, okay?

He says, "Grab this towel." He says, "Stand up and grab it." He says, "Can't you stand?" Then he picks me up and carries me over to the curb. Mr. Capote, you should have been there for you to hear this great voice of his! Meaning, no kidding, Bill Lido shouting "Taxi! Taxi!"

Guess what. I bet we went by your place on the way. For what it's worth, I think we did. Hey, did present company have his residence in Gotham back then? Whereas be serious, when it comes to your so-called tallest building you-know-where, yours truly could definitely tell you which one it was back in that day and age!

I said, "It's snowing." But maybe I was sleeping. On the other hand, I think I said, "It's snowing." It was very sleepy-feeling for me, the snow and the steam and all of these other things—like the towel so floppy-feeling, for example.

He said, "There's paper and pencil in your lap. Write down your family's telephone."

I said, "Is this on account of Buddy Brown?"

It makes me feel like I have to sit here and cry. I mean, how Bill Lido had his arm around me and had the towel.

So could a certain somebody ask you something? Meaning, the title—so is it or isn't it okay if yours truly just goes ahead and leaves the whole entire subject of what is the title to give it all up to guess who?

Meanwhile, somebody says, "Lift up."

Somebody gets me by the wrist and bends my arm out.

Somebody says, "This youngster."

There's light. It is like there is all the light.

Somebody says, "That's right. That's good."

Somebody says, "That's got it. That's good."

Somebody says, "Very good, very good."

YOU KNOW WHAT I SAY?

I say they come in and ask you this, that, and the other thing, okay? But do they tell you the name of the place you are in? Or, hey, or even how long you have been in the place? On the other hand, this is something yours truly can definitely assure present company of, which is that it is not in (joke) in Gotham, ha ha! I don't know. I mean, I know a certain individual has to know about this type of thing for the book when he has to sit himself down to type it up. But I'll be honest with you, it is not like you-know-who is holding anything back! The other thing is, they come in and ask you the questions. Or they come in and they say to you, you know, "Drink it." Or they come in and show you the thing with the laces. I'm serious—this in a nutshell is the whole thing of it right there!

Except for Everett and his icebreakers.

Like suppose you said to Everett, "Why is it they have the mats on the walls?" So then Everett says, "Who says there are mats on your walls?" Or suppose you said to Everett, "Why is it they put me in here?" So then Everett says, "Everybody has got to be some place." But his biggest icebreaker of all was when Everett said not one person in millions and millions of people was lucky enough not for them not to be born!

That's Everett.

Everett had all of these different icebreakers of his for yours truly. You know what Everett was? Everett was what T.C. would call a so-called card! "Lord, Lord."

Yours truly kept his eye on the leaves.

This is what yours truly did all of the way down on the train with you-know-who to Gotham. He watched the leaves. He watched them until you couldn't see them anymore because of the buildings in the way and then the tunnel. The next thing was Pennsylvania Station! You know what a certain individual said to himself? He said, "It's a small world." Here's why. Because being in Pennsylvania Station made me think of the program! Hey, doesn't present company remember the one they called *Grand Central Station*? So did this make sense or did this make sense? Because let's not sit here and forget who was on that one and all those others of them back in the days he was still a famous celebrity on the radio!

She says, "For your information, did anybody have a choice? Whereas in my personal opinion, they worked a miracle." She says, "Believe me, you should get down on your hands and knees, and thank God for what they did for you up there in that place because, don't kid yourself, they worked a miracle." She says, "I promise you, if you are waiting for me to apologize to somebody, then I say don't hold your breath." She says, "If you want my advice, you had a lesson coming to yourself and a certain somebody got it, take it or leave it." She says, "You think anybody is ever forgetting so fast all of the heartache you put me through with this, that, and the other thing, not to mention guess who vanishing into thin air, end of discussion, period?" She says, "Believe me, I am here to tell you, I have got not one thing in the world for me to sit here and be ashamed of." She says, "So did you run me a merry chase or did you run me a merry chase?" She says, "Forget it, a call out to Jersey is next to nothing when you look at what you cost me in sleeplessness and in heartache from, I promise you, from the word go." She says, "You're all wet if you are sitting there looking at you-know-who and pointing a finger." She says, "Just between you, me, and the lamppost, yours truly did you a favor."

I said, "I think I have to go to the bathroom."

She says, "Granted, people have to go."

I said, "It's okay. I'll only be a minute."

She says, "Here." She says, "Take this." She says, "Everybody should always have a dollar in their pocket."

So this is what I had. Whereas I don't have to tell you, they didn't get any of your big money for the subway back in that day and age! Not to mention constant bodily harm all of the time! Don't kid yourself, T.C. is scared to death to get on and ride on them. To tell you the truth, this is one subject which yours truly has to go along with T.C.'s thinking on!

I HAD TO WAIT ALL DAY for her to come out. But it was okay. I liked seeing the leaves everywhere and seeing this brand-new borough for me. Believe me, it made a certain person very proud in his own right for him to see the caliber of school which Janet R. went to! On the other hand, I can't say it looked like its name. But yours truly can't say anything which does! So am I right or am I right? Like take a camisole! Or let's face it, who was Binny?

I just ran when I saw her!

I just ran for Janet R.!

I said, "My beloved, my beloved!"

She said, "You."

Then she said some other things which in my personal opinion are no good as quotes for the book.

"How come you don't have the same face as before?"

"Didn't anybody tell you you don't have the same face as before?"

"How come they changed your face so that it's not the same face as before?"

Hey, here are some firsts for you!

I got to carry Janet R.'s books for her! I got to see Janet R. walking in the leaves! I got to see the Bronx High School of you-know-what!

She said, "Maybe it was the bottle that did it."

She said, "Did they say it was the bottle that did it?"

She said, "Do you think it was the bottle that did it?"

Mr. Capote, I have to tell you something—yours truly did not have any answers for her, end of discussion, period!

"Red Dog, Red Dog, this is Blue Dog calling! Do you read me, do you read me, please?"

LISTEN, I HAVE TO ASK YOU SOMETHING. What if we call it quits right here! I mean, with just the twenty-three! So you tell me, was the one with the bike the limit or was the one with the bike the limit? On the other hand, I can see where it is probably a pretty touchy subject, yours truly making to present company a brand-new recommendation like this.

It is just the fact that to a certain someone's way of

thinking, maybe you-know-who bit off more than he can chew. Let's face it, sometimes your eyes (joke) are bigger than your stomach, ha ha. But seriously, you think we could work out a deal on maybe twenty-three instead of, you know, instead of forty-seven? Okay, no reason for us to actually sit down and talk turkey yet, but since when does it hurt for an individual to throw out a few ideas before getting down to brass tacks? For instance, what would you say to this, which is twenty-four instead of twenty-three? You see what I am saying? In other words, the next one, we make the next one, you know, *capstone*. So let's say *capstone* comes next! Because I'll be honest with you.

I'm tired.

Whereas here's another thing.

Meaning, this thing which has come up with people sticking things on the refrigerator again!

"Red Dog, Red Dog, please come in!"

Believe me, no offense. You know what I say? I say is business business, or is business business? Look, yours truly knows he does not have to tell you forty-seven is definitely as of now out of the question as of now! So are we talking turkey or are we talking turkey? Because God is my judge, the thing which just dawned on me is one for the books!

Face facts, credit where credit is due. Didn't a certain individual say you were a top man? So would anybody expect anything different from a top man? Believe me, yours truly would be the first one to say to you your top man does not get to be a top man just from him sitting around twiddling his thumbs, okay? In other words, your top man has to look out for himself! Am I right or am I right? I mean, come on, yours truly was definitely not born yesterday!

You want to hear something crazy? Trees! I mean, saying Peartree's all of the time and thinking about Peartree's all of the time just reminded me! Which is of how there were trees outside of the window outside of Sylvia Berman's! Hey, I was so dumb in that day and age! Except for Davie was always going out and getting mud on him—whereas look at guess who inside with the radio! But take you. Or take Norman. I mean, you take any of your top men and what's the answer? The answer is your top men were not listening to the radio instead of the teacher! Come on, be honest with me, this is how everybody gets to be a top man, true or false? Don't kid me, top men of the future sitting around listening to any vacuum or people in the public going jingle, jingle, jingle, nibble, nibble, nibble! So am I talking turkey or am I talking turkey?

This is why I tell T.C. when it comes to the question of the boy's educational experiences, she is all wet from the word go! Granted, granted, T.C. says, "Lord, Lord." But I say who is the father of the boy? And for your information, I'll tell you something else! I'm sorry but this is who the father of the boy is! You heard me, this is who! And another thing—you think Buddy Brown ever had to only wait a minute? Because don't kid yourself! When it comes to people in the public throwing paper, no Buddy Brown ever had to hear that! Not to mention opening a closet and seeing them tell you they were dancing! You know what? Buddy Brown could sleep!

Wait a minute! Did I tell you about *yowsah, yowsah, yowsah?* I can't remember if I told you. In other words, in the Old Maestro's sign-off, he said *yowsah, yowsah, yowsah* instead of saying yes sir, yes sir, yes sir!

Oh, Mr. Capote, she was so wonderful. I saw her walking in the leaves! *Did you ever see a lassie go this way and that way and this way and that way?* Oh, Mr. Capote, please!

"Red Dog, Red Dog! Answer me, please!"

SHE SAID, "COME OVER HERE with me and stand here with me in the mirror with me."

Here is something.

The apartment was very nice. It was nicer even than Mrs. Hirsch's was. You know what? Sylvia Berman looked like Sue Cott looks. In other words, Channel 2, check it out!

Listen, did yours truly make mention of where he used to call color at the top concession? Okay, it was just Long Beach on Long Island and not in Gotham, but don't kid yourself, this doesn't make it not a top one!

Hey, I was just thinking of something. What if they came in and asked Davie the questions? Correction: That wasn't what yours truly was thinking of!

Here's something else.

She says, "Syl! Is that you, Syl?"

On the other hand, you take pulmotor. Or somebody saying, "Drink it." Or, hey, "What is the tallest building in New York City?" You know what I say? Yours truly says blame it on the channels! She says, "Jesus Harold Christ, will you hurry!" She says, "Look at you in the mirror."

It's like Paki! It's like what comes out is not what you expected. You know what it's like? It's like Paki went crazy!

She says, "Syl! I'm calling you, Syl!"

She says, "I am sick and tired of you in here watching every move I make." She says, "Go outside and play!"

Hey, false alarm!

Listen, I am going to be honest with you. Guess who's got quotes for him to give you for the book galore!

HEY, TIME OUT! I THINK I AM too tired to think. It's this writing thing. Because a certain individual has to hand it to you, sitting down and typing it up! You know what? As God is my judge, she says, "Hold the phone."

Just think of it. This gick going plop on the bicycle seat. Plop plop plop. Or Buddy Brown, for instance. Splat. Whereas if you are still up there where he was before he started falling, it's, you know, it's woof woof woof.

You want to hear the payoff? The messenger who was on her way over to your place today? No gears! Take it or leave it, no gears. I'm sorry, I'm serious. Not even three speeds! But what's the diff? Hey, a flat tire, my (joke) eye, ha ha!

Listen, I'll tell you who had speeds.

You want to know who had speeds?

The answer is Buddy Brown!

Not even with a bicycle, ha ha!

SHE SAYS, "SYL!"

She says, "Syl, come on, Syl! "

Oh, Mr. Capote, I think I'm getting another one. No kidding, I think I am probably getting probably the world's biggest boner!

She says, "Sylvia, I am calling you!"

She says, "Him and me are clearing the hell out!"

She starts getting a little sweaty. Her face gets different and sweaty. It sounds like this. It sounds like a click. I can hear it go click. There is this sweaty thing all over her. It's like it makes her change all over her.

I said, "Oh, my beloved, please!"

LISTEN, I AM JUST GOING TO LET my hair down with you. So is it okay if yours truly lets his hair down with you? Because it's high time we talked turkey! Meaning, you-know-who was in the house listening to the radio!

Ask Davie.

"What is the tallest building in New York City?"

Ask Davie!

I said, "Who is Binny? Or Sylvia Berman?"

She said, "You should get down on your hands and knees and thank God that this block has such a nice boy for everybody to play with."

Hey, time out!

I need some deep ones.

Okay, I'm breathing.

Okay, taking some more deep ones!

"Red Dog! Come in, Red Dog, come in!"

You think it's easy to be in Simon's? You think it's easy for you to drink it when they come in with it and say for you do it? You think it's easy for you to stick it in when there's this gick that comes bubbling up out of it?

"Red Dog, come in, Red Dog, come in! This is Blue Dog calling Red Dog—come in, Red Dog, come in!"

I said, "Oh, my beloved, please!"

So you tell me, does it make any sense or does it make any sense?

I mean, the Empire State Building, please!

"Red Dog! Red Dog! This is an emergency, Red Dog Please! answer me, Red Dog, please!"

Ask Davie.

"Red Dog, Red Dog, Red Dog!"

She says, "Will you quit it with that shit and get my show on the TV, please!"

You hear it?

Click.

She says, "It's gorgeous out. Go out and play!"

She says, "Hold the phone, goddamn it! Can't you see I'm getting ready to turn?"

No kidding, her face got different. It was getting pretty sweaty and different!

I have a boner now! I have a boner!

Did I tell you about the number on Paki? Believe me, if I told you, present company would be sorry if yours truly did.

I remember a room. I remember a mirror.

T.C. says, "Syl?"

Somebody says, "In here!"

Somebody says, "In here?"

She says, "Could you eat this child up alive or could you eat this child up alive?"

Somebody says, "I'm tired of counting. I'm sick and tired of always counting."

It was such a quiet place. You could hear everything in it if you tried to. Think of the boys on Fourteenth. Think of the paper flopping. Do you hear the paper flopping?

Somebody says, "Is he ridick or is he ridick?"

She says, "Lord, Lord, the pissant is nothing but mouth and no dick!"

She says "God is my witness, a face like an angel!"

She says, "Look in the mirror. You see in the mirror?"

She says, "Come on, son, let's see you lay some pipe!"

He says, "The rhumba, the mambo—you name it, kiddo—we could really do it!"

"Red Dog! It's Blue Dog calling! Come in!"

What number are we up to, true or false?

Okay, time out, deep breaths!

You should see the number they put on Paki!

Did you ever see a lassie go this way and that way and this way and that way?

Oh, my beloved!

You-know-who is stopping for a time-out. A certain person is stopping for a time-out. Okay, time out!

Somebody says, "What's a pulmotor?"

Somebody says, "Piss off!"

I said, "What?"

Somebody says, "Get out of my face, you faggot jerk!"

I said, "What?"

Somebody says, "Don't hand me that what shit! I been watching you watch me! Go watch somebody else!"

I said, "I work in a bank." I said, "This is the direction I am going in." I said, "For your information, it just so happens we are two people both going in this direction."

Somebody says, "I'm counting to three, man—I'm counting one, I'm counting two . . ."

I said, "It is called Peartree's." I said, "I am just on my way to lunch at Peartree's." I said, "Ask anyone." I said, "Ask Davie." I said, "Ask all of the people."

Somebody says, "I'm telling you for the last time, pansy—fuck off or I'll beat your little ass but good!"

I said, "Amentia."

Or I said, "Illaudable."

She said, "What?"

Click.

Granted, first there was the runny stuff no different than the rest! But then God should strike me dead, you would not believe your eyes what starts coming out next! So do you see what I'm saying or do you see what I'm saying?

"Red Dog! This is Blue Dog! Emergency! Emergency!"

She says, "Go play." She says, "You will never find a nicer child to play with you." She says, "So go play."

She says, "There ain't no little pitchers with no ears!"

Just kidding.

Just breaking the ice some more.

Hint: Is a certain somebody sitting in a certain fabulous restaurant with a certain unauthorized author breaking bread together with him? Not to mention with also two particular individuals which just so happen to be the other two members of my particular household! Am I right or am I right?

She said, "Higher! Higher! Go all the way in!"

Somebody said, "Oh, you know what paraldehyde is."

Somebody said, "Is that what a pulmotor is?"

I said, "What?"

I said, "What?"

She said, "Faster, higher, faster, higher—in higher faster in, will you please?"

She said, "Don't you dare hand me anymore of that shit-for-brains bullshit! You never offed nobody nor was never on no radio neither!"

She said, "So give it to Syl if your arm's too tired!"

I said, "Oh, my beloved, please!"

She said, "Were you up in that house or were you up in that house, true or false?"

She said, "Okay, faggot, I am counting to three!"

Did you ever see a lassie go this way and that way and this way and that way?

She says, "Two!"

They said, "We are going to ask you three questions."

I said, "Who's Binny?"

She said, "Come over here and just look at this picture."

She said, "Mother of God, talk about runts!"

They said, "Number one."

She said, "Oh. Oh. Oh. Oh."

She said, "Come in here in this kitchen here!" She said, "Take a look up on that refrigerator!" She said, "Is that a picture-book boy or is that a picture-book boy?"

They said, "It is just a question we ask the people."

She says, "All right, three! Now scat, you little creep!"

She says, "You and your goddamn Ben Bernie every goddamn minute of every goddamn minute!"

They said, "It is really very simple. What is your name, how old are you, and what is the tallest building in New York? Now, please. Now, you mustn't keep us waiting, please. You see what Everett has if you do? So let's not have any unpleasantness, please. Or name a city. Would you like to name a city? Pick a city. Just name a city. Try for us. Just try for us. Then you can drink this and then you can have a nice, nice, long, long, good and sleepy sleep."

"Red Dog!"

They said, "Everett, if you please?"

Listen, just between you, me, and the lamppost, I can see the refrigerator from here!

"Red Dog!"

Tell the truth, doesn't it give you a boner when I talk about you-know-who? I promise you, you can tell me. Go ahead and let your hair down! You think this was the thing of it with Norman? You think it was on account of how Mr. M. was always getting these boners whenever yours truly made mention to him of Janet R.? Listen, when André comes over to the table, you ask him what his personal opinion is. Except only if you can get T.C. to cover up both of a certain somebody's ears! Another thing is this—ask Norman who told him about Ann Shepherd and who she really is! Okay, so she was on her way over to your place—so let's face it! So number one, no telling what you could have caught from this person! Number two, whatever you figure it cost you in so many dollars and cents, yours truly says let's go ahead and cut it out of Norman's various different percentages! So you see the direction of my thinking? In other words, the way guess who sees it is this. If the man would have played ball with me in the first place, the mental picture would have been a completely different mental picture! The other thing is, this individual is a family man. So is he any stranger to the situation a family man gets in?

Tell the truth, is the boy there? Because the way yours truly sees it, isn't it way past his bedtime? So did you or didn't you order a Roy Rogers for you-know-who? Because I personally would not want him getting no Shirley Temple, you know! Enough said or enough said?

No kidding, can I really level with you? I mean, speaking as one famous celebrity to another? Because I am here to tell you, a certain person's arm can't take much more of this with this pencil! Hey, yours truly really has to take his hat off to present company, not to mention Norman! Come on, you fellows must have some real arms on you from writing (joke) all of those bestsellers, ha ha! No offense, but don't forget—T.C. is a married woman!

Forget it. I was just kidding.

Believe me, nobody is pointing any finger.

Granted, to her way of thinking, she thinks she has her reasons. In other words, it's a free country. The woman wants to deal with the top men direct, then she wants to deal with the top men direct. You know what I say? I say more power to her! Except you get a couple of sidecars in her, look out, okay? But I'll be honest with you. Where yours truly is concerned, let's face it, where's his head for business? Granted, T.C. is no Gothamite, but does she have a head on her shoulders or does she have a head on her shoulders?

Hey, yours truly sends his regards to André. Which goes ditto for Norman, okay? Let's face it, bygones is bygones! It's all water under the bridge. God is my judge, I am serious, no hard feelings!

"Red Dog! Red Dog! Can you read me?"

Tell the truth. Is that a boy or is that a boy? Could they eat him up alive or could they eat him up alive? I mean, go ahead and talk about a face! Listen, just between you, me, and the lamppost, you are looking at some face! Listen, the way it is working out, guess who says it is better for all parties concerned! I mean, face facts, yours truly can see where he made the wrong start in the first place. In other words, a certain individual would be the first to admit it, I probably should have started with a different start!

Be honest with me. Is Johnny there in the bargain?

You know what?

It made me afraid for them to be asking me questions like that. True or false, wouldn't it make you?

I said, "Please do not ask me questions like that."

They said, "Everett?"

They said, "Everett?"

I'll bet it's getting light out. I'll bet it really is. You can't tell from this kitchen here because in this kitchen there is no window in it. But you know what? I bet it definitely is!

I'm so tired.

It's so fast.

"Red Dog!"

They said, "Here. Like this. Just drink it down fast."

I thought she is in a place where knives are!

I said, "Why are those on the walls?"

They said, "Like this. Just do it fast."

I thought Buddy Brown.

They said, "Don't make us have to make you."

I said, "Just give me a minute to catch my breath."

I was on the hassock watching.

I said, "It has the same laces! It has the same sleeves!"

I said, "Just let me catch my breath!"

They said, "Count to three. Then take a breath."

I was seven, going on eight. Wasn't I always on the hassock? Isn't this where there was a radio? Little things came and went. She moved things and made them make a wave in them.

They said, "One."

They said, "Two."

They said, "Take the pulmotor down to the basement!"

"Oh, Red Dog—oh, my beloved, please!"

HEY, YOU THINK I DON'T KNOW this paper has been looking at me? The whole time a certain somebody has been sitting here doing this, you think he did not know the paper has been doing it? Listen, don't flatter yourself! You-know-who is no Davie! Face facts, will you! Guess who's got eyes in his head! My God, you know what all of you are? You are just me talking to myself instead of me not talking!

You hear me, T.C.? You took him away! But you are just me and he is just me and when yours truly signs off, you are all of you nothing! You hear me, all of you sons of bitches in your fancy famous places? How about it, you people? Turn on the seven-watter!

"Red Dog, I beg you, my beloved, please!"

Forget it! You are all anybody! You are all just one person which leads to another!

Oh, you sons and sons and sons of bitches!

Look at this.

Will you look at this?

Because it is one three zero three zero!

Didn't I tell you, live and learn?

So who is going to say where *capstone* went when you-know-who gets to the day that the word is not there?

"Binny! I beg you! Please answer your father, please!"

Hey, here's looking at you, Mr. Ben Bernie! You went away just like the rest of them did, but I never stopped loving you ever!

Hey, Davie, here's mud in your eye!

Meaning, chapter and verse, enough said?

Now open wide, my Davie, sweet Davie—yours truly, end of discussion, period!

P.S. *And now the time has come to lend an ear to—au revoir, pleasant dree yums—think of us when requesting your thee yums—until the next time when possibly you may tune in again, keep the Old Maestro always in your schee yums—yowsah, yowsah, yowsah—au revoir—may good luck and happiness, success, good health, attend your schee yums—and don't forget, should you ever send in your requesta, we'll try to do our besta, yowsah, yowsah, yowsah—au revoir, a fond cheerio, a bit of a tweet-tweet—and good-night and God bless you*

and pleasant

dree yums